Jax didn't want to h

This place, this farm, this ~~family had too many~~ needs. He could handle any one of them and maintain his distance, but to face all three?

That would call to the protector in him, a side he'd buried when he'd lost four good men to an accident that should never have happened.

He needed to walk away. They'd get by, one way or another. Folks always did.

But when Libby drew the little girl in, laughing about the wind, and shrugging off the blown-down barn as if it was no big deal, he realized he had no choice.

He tugged his faded army cap into place. "I'm going to let this wind ride itself out, then I'll be back."

Libby frowned. "What? Why?"

"To help." He brushed one finger to the brim of his hat. "I'll be here first thing in the morning." He turned, not waiting for permission that might not come.

Multipublished bestselling author
Ruth Logan Herne loves God, her country, her family, dogs, chocolate and coffee! Married to a very patient man, she lives in an old farmhouse in Upstate New York and thinks possums should leave the cat food alone and snakes should always live outside. There are no exceptions to either rule! Visit Ruth at ruthloganherne.com.

Books by Ruth Logan Herne

Love Inspired

Golden Grove

A Hopeful Harvest

Shepherd's Crossing

Her Cowboy Reunion
A Cowboy in Shepherd's Crossing
Healing the Cowboy's Heart

Grace Haven

An Unexpected Groom
Her Unexpected Family
Their Surprise Daddy
The Lawman's Yuletide Baby
Her Secret Daughter

Visit the Author Profile page
at Harlequin.com for more titles.

A Hopeful Harvest

Ruth Logan Herne

HARLEQUIN® LOVE INSPIRED®

Recycling programs
for this product may
not exist in your area.

 LOVE INSPIRED BOOKS

ISBN-13: 978-1-335-42937-7

A Hopeful Harvest

www.Harlequin.com

Printed in U.S.A.

But the wisdom that is from above
is first pure, then peaceable, gentle, and easy
to be intreated, full of mercy and good fruits,
without partiality, and without hypocrisy.
And the fruit of righteousness is sown in peace
of them that make peace.
—*James* 3:17–18

To our fledgling prayer group: I love you all, and what a joy it's been knowing you and praying with you. Aren't we blessed with the fruitful harvest of faith and healthy children? God is good... And He certainly blessed me when He put you all into my life.

Chapter One

Mortgage. Electric bill. Car payment. Gasoline. Milk. Bread. Eggs.

That was as far as Liberty Creighton's budget would stretch until the apple crop came in. She measured ingredients for the tank sprayer, added water and got ready to drive the aging tractor along the expanse of trees in Golden Grove, Washington. Recent rains meant additional spraying to guard against worms and disease.

Was she foolish to take this on to fulfill her late grandmother's wishes to keep Gramps on the farm? Or was it an act of kindness?

She wasn't sure, but she was on the cusp

of her first solo harvest. Their winter budget depended on these final weeks and she and her five-year-old daughter had spent the last year in a town that used to scorn her. Maybe still did. That was their problem. Not hers. Except it still hurt, so maybe it was her problem after all.

She'd completed the Fujis and Galas when the calendar app on her phone buzzed a reminder. She stared at it, dismayed. Lunch with your best girl, twelve o'clock, Golden Grove Elementary!

She was a mess. She hadn't bothered to shower or get dressed in regular clothes because somehow she'd marked her kitchen calendar for lunch with CeeCee tomorrow. Not today.

Maybe the app was wrong.

She knew better as she raced for the house. If she skipped the much-needed shower, threw on clean clothes and hurried to the school…

The clock said 12:05 p.m. when Libby flew back down the stairs. Gramps was snoring in his recliner. She wanted to tell him she was leaving, but she'd have to wake him and deal with his growing disorientation and there was no time for that.

She scribbled a quick note instead. "Lunch at school with CeeCee. Back soon." She put it on his little side table. The table used to be cluttered with pills and random items. She'd reorganized it when she moved in and the order seemed to help Gramps's cognition. He didn't seem as confused with her there, managing things.

She dashed out the door, got in the farm truck and turned the ignition key. It started on the first try.

Thank You, sweet Lord!

She breathed the prayer as she headed for school, trying to ignore the dashboard clock. By the time she pulled into the parking lot, it was 12:19 p.m. She hurried to the door and hit the call button.

No one answered.

She pressed it again as precious seconds drained away.

The door buzzed. She went inside.

"Sign in here, please." An elderly woman stood alongside the security desk inside the door. "And state your business."

"Lunch with my daughter." She spoke brightly as she scribbled her name in the log. When she spun to go, the old woman frowned and stuck out a hand. "Time in, please."

Libby wrote the numbers *12:21* as quickly as she could, then rushed to the cafeteria. She homed in on the clatter of children and lunch trays. She darted through the first set of double doors and scanned the room.

Kids of all sizes were milling around. Adults were overseeing groups of tables, and while she knew CeeCee's teacher, Libby had no idea who the lunch monitor was for her class. She moved to the right, toward the smallest children, and spotted CeeCee as the monitor called them to attention. "Mrs. Reynolds's kindergarteners, time to take care of your garbage and recyclables and line up."

She got to CeeCee's side as her little girl stood up to clean her area. "Hey, girl-friend!"

"Mommy!" Pure joy lit CeeCee's face. She threw her arms out and half jumped into Libby's arms. "I knew you'd come! I knew it! I told everyone that my mom would never forget about me." She turned back toward the gathering children. "Here she is! This is my mommy!"

The lunch monitor didn't try to hide her frown or sound all that sincere. "That's wonderful, darling. She can walk us back to the classroom. Won't that be special?"

Her tone said it wasn't all that special, and her sour expression indicated that Libby fell short in this woman's estimation. *Don't let her push your buttons. Keep your chin in the air and own the moment.*

Libby longed to take the woman down a peg. Clasp CeeCee's hand and sign her out for the afternoon and make the whole day special to make up for her mistake. She couldn't, though. She had work waiting, work that had been put off for too long already. On top of that, Gramps couldn't be left on his own for long periods of time, so that meant she'd walk CeeCee to her class, kiss her goodbye and go back to her orchard chores.

"Mommy, thank you for coming!" CeeCee hugged her again, as if popping in for five minutes was enough.

It wasn't, but she thanked God for her daughter's understanding heart. "You're welcome, darling. I'll see you when you get home, okay?"

"'Cept you don't have a home." One of CeeCee's classmates spoke up, a little girl. "CeeCee said you don't have a home so she lives with her grandpa. Right?"

"No home, for real?" An adorable boy shot dark eyebrows up in surprise. "Then you can come and stay with us, CeeCee, with me and my dad. And my big sister! I would like that a lot!" Excitement widened his smile and Libby fell in love with him instantly.

"Except we do have a home." She squatted low and made eye contact with the kids, including the girl who called CeeCee out. "With my grandpa on the apple farm. We moved here to raise apples and pears and plums and to help CeeCee's great-grandpa get around."

"But we didn't have a home before, did we, Mommy? When we were in that other place and they made us move. Right?" There was no denying CeeCee's earnest request for honesty.

An old ache hit Libby's heart.

Should she admit they'd been homeless? Or gloss over it? Nowhere in the parenting books did the experts explain what to do when your abusive ex-husband bleeds money from your accounts and leaves you bruised and penniless without a roof over your head.

She wanted to brush it off.

She didn't. She faced CeeCee and nodded. "We did have to move, didn't we? And then Ms. Mortie called me to say Gramps and Grandma needed help. We headed up here the very next day. It's cool how God worked things out, isn't it?" She smiled at the class as the teacher came forward to direct them into the kindergarten room. "Just when they needed us, we needed them right back."

"'Xactly!" CeeCee kissed her goodbye and skipped into the room, totally happy. She didn't understand the scourge of homelessness.

Libby did.

But she would never again fall victim to a man's deceit. She'd been foolish once. She would never be foolish again.

The wind came out of nowhere. One minute former army captain Jax McClaren was heading toward his solitary cabin in the hills, and the next, his pickup truck was broadsided by a gust of wind so strong that it thrust the heavy-duty 4x4 sideways.

He gripped the wheel, then fought to maintain his forward progress.

The wind had other ideas.

Military training clicked in. He reduced his speed, eased on the brakes and kept the wheel straight. The brakes created instant friction to help keep the tires under *his* control. Not the wind's.

He edged his way back to the proper side of the road as another car approached, heading west. When the wind slammed again, he narrowly missed sideswiping the smaller car.

His phone chose that moment to indicate a weather warning. "Approaching low front," advised the digitized voice. "Expect dangerously high winds."

He could have used the warning ninety seconds earlier.

The wind played tug-of-war for control of the truck. He was between towns. He'd left Golden Grove after finishing a job for a kindhearted widow who liked to bake him cookies. He had every intention of heading back to his solitary cabin to soak up some peace and quiet. Away from people. Away from gratitude he didn't deserve. Away from life.

But when the wind slammed him again, he wasn't sure he was going to make it. As that took hold, he realized two things more. An old man, wearing nothing but boxer shorts and a T-shirt, was walking down the road, trying to block the raging wind with an inside-out umbrella. Behind him, not far from a bungalow-style house in need of attention, a wooden barn literally blew apart.

Jax didn't blink. Didn't think. He just pulled to the side of the road and jumped out of the truck, directly in the old man's path.

His actions startled the man. White hair flying in the gale-force winds, the old fellow stepped back in alarm.

Jax had lost a grandmother to Alzheimer's nearly a dozen years before. He'd watched the disease drain her mind. Her joy. Her attitude. And her caring. But while others grew impatient with Grandma Molly's changeable faces, he wouldn't. Couldn't. Through the long years of decline, he'd focused on one thing: that she was the same grandmother who helped raise three little boys when they lost their mother. He knew she loved them to the very end. She just didn't remember it.

Recalling that, he used his most respectful tone as he faced the confused wanderer. "I thought I'd give you a lift to wherever it is you're going, sir."

"You know where I'm going?" queried the old guy as if hoping for a positive response.

"I expect we'll figure it out," Jax replied.

"Sounds like a plan!" The old fellow tried to move toward the truck but the wind bested him. Jax took his arm gently and steered him toward the truck door.

A car was coming their way from the east.

Farther out, another car was fighting its way up the road from the west. He helped the man into the passenger side of the truck,

then hurried around to reclaim the driver's seat. He thrust the truck into gear and
started forward. "Were you going home?
Or leaving home?" He shot the aged man
a comforting look and didn't once mention
the lack of attire, but inside he was seeth-
ing.

Who would leave a sick, elderly person
alone like this? Who would let him out
of the house wearing nothing but under-
clothes? If a parent allowed a child to wan-
der like this, they'd be arrested.

The old man pointed toward the bun-
galow just beyond the destroyed barn. "I
reckon I know that place."

"That's where you came from?" Jax
asked. He had to speak up over the roar
of the wind. It raged through the trees and
whooshed beneath the truck. He signaled a
left turn just as an oncoming car signaled a
right turn into the same driveway. "Looks
like you have company, sir."

The word *sir* made the old man smile. "I
could use a bit of company now and again,

but my missus won't be happy about bein' surprised. She likes the house just so when company comes by. That whole 'cleanliness bein' next to Godliness' thing, you know. That's a woman thing, I expect."

Jax wouldn't know. He'd been steering clear of God, family and women and anything that smacked of commitment or caring or real emotion. Surface stuff he could handle since leaving Iraq. Anything deeper than that sent him on to the next job. The next task. The next neighborhood. Offering his help but never his heart. He pulled to a stop as a middle-aged woman exited the car next to him. The insignia on her door indicated she was from a local home health care agency.

She looked from the old man to him, then the flattened barn and let out a low whistle. "What's happened here, Cleve? Where's Libby?" She included both men in the question as the wind helped push them toward the house.

Jax lifted his shoulders. "Don't know. I

found him walking down the road alone as the barn blew apart. I'm Jax McClaren."

"Carol Mortimer, from the home health service in Wenatchee. Folks call me Mortie. Come on, my friend, I can't be taking your pulse or blood pressure out here, now can I?"

Her question seemed to confuse the old man further.

She took hold of one of his arms. Jax took the other, and together they tried to guide him into the side door of the house.

He had other ideas. "I promised I'd keep a lookout," he told them, and for a thin fellow, when he dug his heels into the soft valley soil, he dug hard.

"We can help," said the woman softly. "It's Mortie, Cleve. You remember me, don't you? Where's Libby? Did she have to go out?"

"Please don't tell me that someone would leave this gentleman on his own." That hiked Jax's blood pressure to new levels.

The wind slammed them. He was just

about to lift the elderly fellow into his arms and carry him into the house when a car pulled into the driveway.

It slid to a quick stop and a woman jumped out. The raging wind wrapped her longish sweater around her, and her light brown ponytail whipped back and forth, but it was her face that caught Jax's attention.

Despair, mixed with a generous serving of worry and determination darkened her blue eyes. Despite that, she was still beautiful like one of those inspirational movie heroines his grandma used to watch.

She ran forward and got right in front of the older man. "Gramps, I think that wind's a little too strong for any more spraying today, don't you?"

The old fellow stopped. Stared. Then he blinked as if he'd just come out of a dark movie theater into the light.

The wind pummeled him.

Wide-eyed, he hurried forward of his own volition now. "What are we doin' out in this?" he shouted as he hustled up the side steps and into the house. "Libby, you know better than to run the tractor in a storm like this, don't you?"

The young woman went right along with his new train of thought. "I do. And I'm pretty sure you taught me to dress properly before going out in gale-force winds."

The old fellow was quick to defend his choice of attire. "Well, I was in a hurry, you know."

The woman—Libby—held the old-timer's gaze but she offered him a pretty smile, lightly teasing. "Do tell."

"I was on the lookout for something."

A quick look of regret flattened her features, but she reengaged the smile swiftly. "Yes, you were. I asked you to watch for CeeCee's bus while I was spraying the orchard. But that doesn't come until later."

"So I didn't miss anything?" He posed the question quickly, as if worried he might have messed up. "I knew it was important, but I might have dozed off in my chair…"

The home health woman brought him a fleecy pair of pajama pants and helped him into them.

"And there was a wicked crash and I woke up and knew I was on the lookout for something, but for what?"

Libby looked around in confusion. "A crash?" She scanned the room and the kitchen beyond.

She went pale. Her eyes went wide. She stared out the back window at a monster-size pile of broken sticks and bricks and huffed out a slow, sad breath. "The barn."

Jax hated to bring more bad news, but he'd already spotted her grandfather outside when the barn went down. So something else had awakened the elderly gentleman. He crossed to the side door, opened it and stepped outside.

A swirl of gravel dust stirred old memories he'd shoved aside. Haboobs. The Iraqi desert sandstorms. Troops hunkered down.

That was then.

This is now.

Determined, he walked to the back of the house. And there it was. A second barn, much smaller, but just as flat. Would the house be next?

The house blocked the wind, allowing him time to give it a quick once-over. Where the barns lay in splintered pieces, the house stood firm and square. It was old, maybe the original structure, even, and craftsmen knew how to put a solid building together back then. No, the house looked solid, if worn.

He drew a breath and walked back inside. The home health nurse was brewing tea in the small kitchen. She raised her brows as he entered. "Bad?"

"Yes."

"Both barns?"

What could he say to make this better? Nothing. He nodded.

"But no one died. Or got hurt," the nurse added as the old man's granddaughter came through the connecting doorway. "It could have been worse."

He turned toward Libby. "Someone could have been hurt. Or killed." He looked toward the living room beyond. "He was walking along the road in his skivvies, dazed and confused because he was all alone."

Her gaze narrowed. The smile he'd found engaging disappeared. "And who are you, exactly?"

"Jax McClaren. I was driving by when I spotted him. And the barn."

"Mr. McClaren…" Carol Mortimer began.

He included the nurse in his look. "When someone is that sick, should they be left alone?"

The nurse made a face. "Some patients are fine on their own for an hour or two. It depends on what stage they're in. In this case, Cleve's been fine for short periods. But seems like we might need to revisit our thinking if he gets riled that easily."

"Having a barn destroyed seventy feet from the nearest window isn't an everyday occurrence." Libby folded her arms and faced him. "We need to remember we're not dealing with a small child but a grown man who thinks he's okay, and some of the time he is. And there's still work to be done because this is a working farm. Mortie—" she moved closer to the home health nurse "—you understand. He doesn't want to go someplace else. It would kill him. Grandma said that time and again. He was born on this place and he's made his wishes clear often enough. He was born here and wants to die the same way. How can I deny him that after all he's done for me?"

"But what if Mr. McClaren hadn't come along when he did?" asked Mortie. "What if Cleve had wandered until a branch hit him? Or an airborne missile from someone's roof or barn speared him?"

"What choice do I have?" The young woman splayed her hands. "He wants to be on the farm. It's his one link to reality, but the barn's gone, the shed's demolished and we should be harvesting the early fruit, except there's no place to put it now. Do I throw in the towel on the harvest and tuck him somewhere safe? Or keep my promise to Grandma and let him have one last season?"

A school bus pulled up to the driveway, leaving the question unanswered.

Libby hurried out, wrapped an arm around a small child and walked her inside.

A woman and child striving to make ends meet on a falling-down farm.

They needed someone who knew construction. Someone who knew apples. And, maybe most important of all, someone who'd cared for an Alzheimer's patient before.

Jax didn't want to help.

This place, this farm, this family had too many needs. He could handle any one of them and maintain his distance, but to face all three?

That called to the protector in him, a side

he'd buried when he'd lost four good men to an accident that never should have happened.

He needed to walk away. They'd get by, one way or another. Folks always did.

But when Libby drew the little girl in, laughing about the wind and shrugging off the blown-down barn as if it was no big deal, he realized he had no choice.

He tugged his faded army cap into place. "I'm going to let this wind ride itself out, then I'll be back."

Libby frowned. "What? Why?"

"To help." He brushed one finger to the brim of his hat. "I'll be here first thing in the morning." He turned, not waiting for permission that might not come. "Miss Mortie. And Miss—" He tipped his gaze down to the little girl.

The little girl didn't cuddle into her mother's side like so many would. She beamed a big smile his way and held up her hand, splaying five little fingers. "I'm CeeCee and I'm this many and Gramps said we could get a dog someday. Won't that be the best fun ever?"

"It sure will."

He trotted down the steps and to his truck.

He shouldn't do this. He knew it. He could pick up the phone, inform his family of the situation, and they'd bankroll whatever was needed, letting him stay away.

Except this time he couldn't.

Was it the old fellow's struggle that drew him? Or the beautiful and determined young woman? Or the guileless child?

All three, he realized as he drove around the semicircular drive.

He'd help. Then he'd leave, like he'd been doing for three long years.

End of story.

Chapter Two

Huge equipment came rolling up the farm driveway at 6:55 a.m. the next morning. CeeCee let out a squeal of delight when she spotted huge Caterpillar treads spinning by the first-floor windows. "Mommy! A monster scooper thing is here! And a truck! Like a really, really big one!"

Libby got to the window in time to see the first machine lumber past. It was followed by a big dump truck. And then another. Within five minutes, the ginormous scoop arm was loading barn scrap into the truck's wide bed.

"I heard a commotion." Gramps came

into the kitchen. The sight of the big machines riled him. "What's going on? Who brought those here? Lib, we've got to stop them!"

"Gramps, it's the fixer guys. We love fixer guys, remember?" CeeCee took his hand and something about the touch of her tiny hand calmed the old fellow. "The big wind knocked down our barns and now they're cleaning it up for us. Isn't that so nice of them?"

Libby had placed a call to the insurance company once Mortie and Jax McClaren had left, but she hadn't heard back from them. They wouldn't just send a team out to start fixing things the next morning, would they?

Jax's extended-cab pickup truck rolled into the driveway right then. The sharp truck gleamed white in the September sun. He parked but didn't come straight for the house. He met with the workers out back, then came their way. Libby met him before he got to the side door. "You did this?" She motioned to the oversize machines churning a hundred and fifty feet away from them.

"Can't rebuild until we've cleared the area, right?"

"Except I haven't even heard back from the insurance agency. How will they know what to settle if they don't see evidence?"

He held up his phone. "Pictures. I took several yesterday. Between those and the building's footprint on the ground—"

"The what?"

"The space a building takes up on the ground is its footprint."

"So the area of the base as opposed to the cubic footage."

He smiled as if she was suddenly talking his language. "Exactly. They can figure that out mathematically. Did you have replacement coverage or cash value?"

She heard Gramps coming through the door and didn't want him upset by too much talk. "Cash value. Which means only the estimated value of the property in current condition gets paid out. Correct?" She didn't have to ask because she'd worried about that all night, hence the dark circles under her eyes. What was it about this guy that made her think about her looks?

"There are ways of making it stretch."

"I can make a fitted sheet stretch. Money's tougher. But you're right," she added as Gramps drew near. "There's always a way to make things work."

"Your grandma said we should get the best insurance we could because old folks like us can't be fixing things on a thin dime, but I told her our policy was fine and look at this!" Gramps stumped his cane against the stone driveway. He remembered to use it fifty percent of the time. The other half he shuffled along, finding a foot grip. "Look how quick they got here. I guess I was right again, eh?"

"You did just fine, sir."

Jax's words and his deferential tone puffed up Gramps's chest.

Libby knew the work crew had nothing

to do with the farm's thin insurance policy, and Jax could have inflated his own ego by taking credit.

But he didn't.

He let an aging dementia patient claim the kudos and seemed fine doing it. What kind of man did that?

A nice one, her conscience scolded. *There are lots of nice people in this world. Stop being jaded.*

There were nice people.

Libby knew that.

But her family's reputation in Golden Grove left a sour taste on a lot of tongues. Her parents hadn't been the raise-your-kid-normal and go-to-church-on-Sunday sort and when Grandma sent them packing, they took the one thing Grandma didn't want them to take.

Her.

Then sent her back with a sack of ill-fitting clothes when they got tired of her eighteen months later.

Folks had looked at her funny then. And

some still looked at her funny, but now she was mature enough to shrug it off. "I've got to get CeeCee ready for school. Gramps, are you going to stay outside and watch the action?"

"Don't mind if I do." He'd set an old hat on his head. He was still in his pajama pants and a faded blue cotton T-shirt, but it was a mild morning. "If Mother comes looking for me, tell her where I am."

"I will." She was never quite sure if she should play along or explain reality to him, and no one seemed to have the answer. This time she played along.

Jax shot her a look of sympathy. The look felt good. As if someone besides Carol Mortimer understood the situation and was on her side, but she'd been fooled by a man before.

Her ex-husband had taught her a valuable lesson about trust. If she and CeeCee went through life as a duo, she was okay with that. She'd been raised by parents who really never cared. CeeCee would never need to say that.

The five-year-old met her at the door. "Look. I got all dressed for school so I can see the fixer guys. Okay?"

"Okay, once you eat breakfast. What'll it be? A bagel or cereal or an apple?"

"Apple!"

"Ginger Gold or Gala?"

"The redder one."

Libby cut the Gala into slices. She'd seen a study online that talked about the amazing health benefit of apples, how modern science proved the old adage "an apple a day" true. How apples were like the perfect food.

They would have lots of apples for the coming months. That was an added bonus of being on the farm. But with the barn gone and the insurance shortfall and the co-pays on Gramps's meds, the already tight situation had just become impossible.

With men this is impossible; but with God all things are possible.

One of Grandma's favorite verses in the Bible. The walls of the house were peppered with cross-stitched Bible verses.

Libby would cling to the idea that all things were possible. She hadn't come back here by choice but by necessity. God had worked that timing out perfectly. So now?

She would put this firmly in His hands because once CeeCee was on that school bus, she had an orchard to spray, and right now she was just real glad she'd parked the tractor outside the barn before it blew down.

The tractor wasn't parked outside the barn.

It was under the barn. Buried. And as the gaping mechanical claw reached in and scooped up a serving of weathered wood, a generous section of the tractor went with it.

Libby couldn't take her eyes from the scene.

She'd parked the tractor here. Right here. At the edge of the driveway leading to the orchard because her phone alarm had star-tled her. And besides, they rarely put the tractor in the big barn except at the end of the season, once the apple sales were com-plete.

Gone.

Demolished.

Emotions didn't just rock her this time. They fought their way for possession, like that giant claw digging through a debris field of shattered hopes and dreams.

Now there was no tractor to lift the crates of apples to the barn storage or the sale bins.

No tank to give that last vital spraying.

No nothing.

Nothing at all.

Was this God's message to her? To tuck Gramps in a safe spot and walk quietly away with CeeCee? Because it was com-ing through loud and clear.

"You okay?" Jax was coming her way and his question brought her up short.

She wasn't all right. She wasn't sure if

she'd ever be all right. But Libby Creighton was a survivor, so she wiped moisture from her cheeks and turned.

Sympathetic gray eyes met hers beneath his military-cut brown hair. Ocean-gray eyes, they were. Not a hint of blue, but not storm gray like yesterday's clouds. Softer. Gentler. She pulled in a deep breath and paused.

Then she blew out the breath and nodded. "Fine. As fine as I can be now that I see the tractor under thousands of pounds of roof and wall debris."

"You didn't know the tractor was in there?" Surprise furrowed his brow.

"Nope." She made a face. "I parked it here when I realized I had to run to CeeCee's school. Right here. There's no way the wind could have pushed it into the barn, is there?"

"Not feasibly."

"Then how?" She paused when she spotted Gramps talking enthusiastically with a very patient dump truck driver. "He must have moved it. After he woke up. Every now and again he'll hop on it as if ready to work. Sometimes it's a chore that needs to be done. Sometimes it's a memory of what he used to do. He must have come out here and moved the tractor before you found him."

"Into the barn. During the windstorm?" Jax looked disbelieving. "Do you know how close he came to being killed?"

His tone stung. She folded her arms, then unfolded them. She'd promised herself she wouldn't cower again. Not now. Not ever. "I do now. I can't imagine what he was thinking."

Jax stared at her, and she read his gaze because no one knew what Gramps was thinking. Or what he might do from moment to moment. It was obvious that Gramps couldn't be left alone anymore. Not even for short periods of time. How was she going to manage that with everything else on her plate?

Libby didn't have a clue.

She turned back toward the cleanup. "We'll make sure someone's with him from now on. We've been seizing the good moments as if they were the norm, but they're not. Not anymore. It's time we faced the fact that now they're the exception."

"I like to see them as a gift."

His words surprised her.

"When we get those moments of lucidity. Of recognition. An hour here or there." A slight wrinkle formed between his eyes. "Like opening a curtain on the past."

"That's exactly what it's like." She faced him more squarely. "He wasn't this bad when I got here last year to see my grandmother through her hospice time. She loved him so much. When she saw what was happening, she made me promise to keep him on the farm as long as possible. To let him find peace among his apples. And then Central Valley Fruit stepped in to buy the farm, Gramps had a mighty row with their sales rep, and Grandma died while they were arguing the merits of small versus big at the top of their lungs. I don't think he's ever forgiven himself for not being at her side when she died. When he remembers, that is."

Central Valley Fruit.

The business his family began when irrigation was approved for the arid valley soil a hundred years ago. Central Valley Fruit was a megaproducer that had helped put Washington State on the map as a premier source of fruits, not just for American stores, but internationally. With European fruit production decreasing, Central Valley Fruit was happy to fill the void. His father had filled him in on their need for more land a few weeks ago, and available land wasn't an easy find. So they'd put in a bid on this farm? Probably so.

"They contacted us again a few weeks ago. They said that our specific location would be especially good for certain apples because of the microclimate of a slope facing southeast."

"And what did you tell them?" He didn't mention that he understood the ins and outs of selective orcharding.

"I didn't say anything. I left it to Gramps because the farm is still in his name, and he was adamant as he told the fruit rep to leave."

"So he left?"

"He did. And he didn't seem insulted. He said…" She paused a moment as if gathering her thoughts. Or maybe her emotions. "He'd give us time to think about it because he understood what a big decision it was. And he left the contract with Gramps, just in case."

That would be Kenneth, his older brother. Kenneth had a heart. But he also had a goal, and if they needed more land, Ken would find it.

"Total world domination of the world's fruit market." That was a tongue-in-cheek corporate goal.

They used to laugh about it but Libby's

expression showed this was not a laughing matter.

The acquisition of land near the Yakima and Wenatchee Rivers was important to the development of new apple types. Not all apples were created equal and microclimates were crucial for production. The microclimate in Golden Grove was ideal for newer cultivars. "Are they offering a fair price?"

"More than fair," she admitted. "Our current cash flow makes it quite tempting. But I made a promise to my grandmother and I never break a promise. Although I don't know how we're going to pull it off without a barn or a tractor."

He swallowed hard.

He should tell her who he was. But then she'd wonder why he was here. Why he was helping. It would look like a setup to get in her good graces.

It wasn't.

It was something to keep him from thinking. From remembering. From seeing that helicopter spin over a Middle Eastern desert, then watch helplessly as it came crashing down.

"Well." She took a step back. "I'm going to call Baker Orchards and see if they'll let me borrow their tractor for this last application on the September fruits. If they're open to that, I can get one thing done."

He nodded.

She didn't have to do this.

She could walk away and no one would criticize her choice because this was an autumn disaster. Her inexperience was either her saving grace or worst enemy, because with no place to store the apples, there was little sense in continuing. "Your grandfather can stay here with me if you need to leave."

That realization changed her expression. Knowing she couldn't just hop in the old pickup truck and run up the road to the Bakers' place, another roadside fruit stand on the opposite side of Golden Grove. "You wouldn't mind? I'd take him but there's no way to bring him back on their tractor. If it's available."

"Don't mind at all."

She pulled out her phone, made the call and was on her way in less than ten minutes.

Gutsy.

Resolute.

And he'd be a stupid man if he didn't add *downright lovely* to the list of attributes.

He wasn't stupid, but Jax knew his limitations. No one wanted any part of the nightmares, cold sweats and sadness that hit him when least expected. He didn't want it, either, but he had little choice. It was his reality.

Little choice?

His conscience upbraided him none too gently.

Allison recommended you for that new treatment. The guy has an office in Seattle. A ninety-minute drive that could make a difference. So why haven't you done it?

Fear? Doubt? Lack of faith in much of anything anymore?

Allison was a solid therapist. She made him think, sometimes too much. He wasn't against getting help, but if nothing worked, why waste time?

He'd come home as damaged goods, but at least he'd come home. Those four men and the chopper pilot never got that chance.

So yeah, the big, brave warrior didn't want to remember but couldn't possibly forget. It wouldn't be right to impose this reality on anyone else, family or friends. And that meant he'd quietly keep on doing what he'd been doing in the lush valley for the last few years. Helping people as he could. And pretending to be someone he wasn't.

For now...

It was enough.

Chapter Three

Libby finished spraying the September fruit acreage just before CeeCee's bus was due, but that brought new problems to the table. CeeCee couldn't be left alone. Libby had lost a couple hours of time by driving Si Baker's John Deere down the two-lane this morning and she had to have the tractor back to him by early the next day. And then there was Gramps.

Who was going to keep an eye on him when she was in the orchard?

She parked the tractor at the edge of the Gala apple rows. She should be picking them now, and she would have been if things had gone all right yesterday.

But they hadn't.

The bus rolled up to the driveway. The door opened and Gert Johnson waved a hand as CeeCee came racing up the short drive to the house. "Libby, we're all so sorry about what happened yesterday! A bunch of us bus drivers will be happy to help with whatever you need. And that includes pickin' apples between bus runs. Call me. Okay?"

"I will, Gert. And thank you." Oncoming cars made her yell the response back because Gert couldn't be holding up traffic. On quiet days it wouldn't matter so much, but during apple harvest season there was no such thing as a quiet day. Harvesters and pickers and trucks rumbled by continuously. In the Columbia Valley, the beautiful words of Ecclesiastes 3 came to life. "To everything there is a season." Right now the season was apples.

"Mommy, look! Look!" CeeCee held up

an unrecognizable picture. She beamed with pride and excitement. "Isn't it so beautiful?"

"It is! I love how you captured the shape, darling."

"Barn shapes aren't real hard," CeeCee told her, having no idea she'd given her mother a solid clue.

"Hard or not, you did a great job. Is this our barn?"

CeeCee shook her head. Her curls bounced as Gramps and Jax came around from the back. The last dump truck was being loaded, then the damaged sites would be scraped clean.

"It's that one." She pointed up the road to the Moyer building. The Moyers had sold their farm to CVF two years before. Their land stretched east but this one lone building hadn't been used for anything except storage for over a dozen years. "See the slopey top?"

"I see it." Jax smiled down at CeeCee.

CeeCee smiled back. "Because you know stuff about barns, maybe."

"A bit."

CeeCee grinned up at him.

He grinned back.

A warning stab hit Libby squarely. She wasn't unfamiliar with how some men toyed with a woman's heart. Been there. Done that. Not pretty.

But no one was going to mess with CeeCee's emotions. Her ex-husband had already done his share of that with his lying and cheating. For years she could have called her life an old-time country song.

Not now.

Now her life would be an hallelujah. Because she had the power within herself to change what she could and shrug off the rest.

"Can you hustle inside and grab a sweatshirt? The Bakers' tractor has a cab, so you can ride with me while I spray," Libby told her.

CeeCee hugged her great grandfather and nodded eagerly. "I love helping!"

Jax stepped forward. He smelled of apples and fall and Washington fresh air. He put out his hand, then set it on her arm. "Let me do the spraying."

Her arm warmed beneath his touch and her pulse skittered.

She hid her reaction and started to refuse, but he dropped his gaze to CeeCee before lifting it to her grandfather. "You'll do better here and I've run a lot of spray arms in my time. Is the tank full?"

She nodded.

"How far did you get?"

"Through the Red Delicious."

"I'll start at the Granny Smiths, then. They've finished the demo removal and I've got nothing going on the rest of the day."

Why was that? she wondered.

But she didn't wonder long because it made sense. "If you really don't mind, that would be wonderful. Then I can get the tractor back to the Bakers and start harvesting tomorrow."

"Glad to help." He'd lost his army cap somewhere and was wearing a faded baseball cap with *USA* in bold letters on the front. He tipped it slightly. "You know where I'll be."

He didn't just walk to the tractor. He strode as if spraying her trees was the most important job ever given.

CeeCee jumped into her arms. "I've got so much to tell you guys because school was so much fun!"

Her genuine delight eased Libby's school concerns.

"Tell me all about it. Gramps, how about if I make you a cup of tea and you can rest awhile?"

"I won't mind it a bit. These feet are tired of standin' watchin' others do the work, but it was some quick work, wasn't it? I told your grandmother that policy would be just fine. I told her."

"You did."

She'd read that green tea helped cognition. She'd read a lot of stuff, but nothing seemed to help Gramps's hastening decline. She brought him the tea and turned the TV on softly. He was asleep in five minutes. By the time Jax rolled the tractor back up the access drive, she had a pot of red sauce ready and water simmering for pasta.

He knocked at the side door. CeeCee rushed to let him in. When she went to hug him, he held back. "Not with spraying clothes on, little lady. Chemicals and kids don't mix." He ignored CeeCee's look of disappointment and called up the side stairs. "Give me your car keys and I'll run the tractor up the road, then bring your car back."

She crossed to the stairs and looked down, right into his eyes. A gaze that hinted at melancholy, much like hers. "You don't have to do that. You've done so much already."

He smiled. "I think a plate of pasta and

whatever sauce you've got cooking makes it even. Don't you?"

Having him stay for supper? Um, no. Small-town single mothers and stray men were not a good mix.

"You can have supper with us? Like, to-night?" CeeCee didn't hug him, but she grasped his hand. "That would be so nice! Wouldn't it, Mommy?"

What could she say without being rude? She wiped her hands on a dry towel, stepped down and handed him her keys. When she did, her hand brushed his. The lightest touch. So why did that minimal contact send her heart beating stronger again? Faster? She drew her hand away quickly. "We'd be honored to have you to supper. Of course."

"I don't have to stay."

He was graciously offering her a way out of the predicament. Because he sensed her hesitation? Or because he disapproved of how she handled Gramps?

Either way, he'd gone the distance for

them today. "Please stay." She lifted her eyes to his as he took a step back toward the gravel drive.

Big mistake. Because she was pretty sure when she looked into his eyes, she saw his soul. A soul that was just as fractured as hers. Then the glimpse was gone, replaced by a smile that seemed well practiced. She knew because she had polished one of those smiles herself.

"Mighty obliged, ma'am." He winked. Then he climbed back onto the tractor, whistling. She couldn't hear the whistle when he started the old John Deere up, but she'd recognized the tune. Gramps used to sing it to her twenty-five years ago, when she'd dash in and around the apple trees. It was their song.

She hummed it now.

Gramps woke up as she put the pasta into the boiling water a few minutes later. He grinned as he came into the kitchen. "Remember how we used to sing that when you were a little girlie?"

"I sure do."

"And then you went off and started sittin' under apple trees with other folks. Not listenin' to your grandma and me."

Every now and again he'd start scolding. It took everything she had not to take offense. He wasn't wrong. They'd tried to warn her about her choices. In a search for someone to love her, she hadn't listened, and every now and again Gramps brought it up. "We all make mistakes, Gramps. Look, I made red sauce. Your favorite."

Trying to change the subject didn't work today. "I told ya. Your grandma tried to talk sense into ya, but kids don't like to listen. We saw what happened with your mother and we didn't want the same thing to happen with you."

She set down the spoon and crossed the room. "I learned my lesson. Now I'm here and we can leave all that behind us. Can't we?"

His brow drew down. His forehead wrinkled. He seemed to be grasping for something to say, but Jax walked in the side door right then.

He seemed to size up the situation quickly. "Sir, can I take you for a short walk to the barn sites? I need your opinion on a couple of things."

"Me? Oh. Sure!" The transformation of Gramps's face was almost instantaneous. "We'll be gettin' the apples in the barn soon, if I can get this girl on some kind of proper schedule."

Kindness deepened Jax's expression when he looked at her. Then he took Gramps's arm and helped him down the three steps to the side door. "Still smells real good in there." He flashed a quick smile her way, but it was a smile tinged with compassion. "How much time do we have?"

"Eight minutes until the pasta's done."

"We'll be back." He led Gramps outside. She breathed.

Minute to minute, she wasn't sure what Gramps would say or do. Remember or forget. She would seek Mortie's advice once

Gramps and CeeCee were asleep. Mortie wouldn't mind her calling after hours. She'd been a good friend to Libby's mother when they were young, before her mother took a walk on the wild side. Mortie would advise and counsel. Never blame. And Libby could use a dose of that wisdom right about now.

Worn down.

That was what he saw when he looked into Libby's dark blue eyes. Eyes that matched the Central Washington sky.

Was she worn down by life? Circumstances? The current situation?

Maybe all three. Which meant he needed to keep his distance like he did on every job. Trouble was, this job was different. If he stayed to help rebuild that barn, he'd be here every day, wanting to help because something in her called to him. The pain she tried to hide. The self-confidence she pretended to have. The hurt he'd seen from something the old fellow said.

Grandma Molly had been the same way.

She'd gotten downright nasty at times, and he'd been one of the few people who saw beyond the curt words. The hurled insults. Because he knew it wasn't her saying those rude things. It was the disease.

He should leave this job to someone else. The family foundation could have the whole thing done as an act of mercy, but then she'd know that it was Central Valley Fruit footing the bill and might refuse their help.

"Them apples, them first ones, they've got to come off those trees now." Cleve gripped Jax's arm with one hand and pointed with the other. "They should be in the barn, and out on the sales tables out front. What's that girl been doin'?" he grumped, then stopped dead to rights. "Where'd the barn go?"

The old fellow's angst made Jax's decision. Yeah, the foundation could rebuild the barn but they couldn't get to the root of the problem. The old man's declining state.

He could. If nothing more than giving her some respite as things got worse. He'd faced this disease with his grandmother with a host of help, professional and family.

Libby had no one but herself and her little girl and the nurse from the local agency. Jax knew the score. This was a 24/7, 365 kind of illness. Two hours a day, three times a week wasn't going to cut it.

He'd see it through.

He'd try to keep his distance from Libby Creighton and her precious daughter. He'd stay civil and kind. That was what they needed right now. Strong hands, a strong back and someone to help with Gramps. He readdressed the orchardist's concern about the barn. "We had a wicked windstorm yesterday, sir."

"Call me Cleve. We're friends, ain't we?"

"I'd like that. Well, Cleve, we had a bad windstorm, as bad as I've seen it get, and it took down the big barn and the smaller one, too. So we got them cleaned up today, and we'll have supplies brought in to start rebuilding soon."

"Supper's ready." CeeCee dashed down

the drive to meet them. "Mommy said to tell you."

Cleve glanced back as they moved toward the house. "Them big trucks came, right?"

Jax encouraged the memory. "They did. They cleared the site for us."

"I told Mother. I told her our insurance policy was plenty good enough and she argued to beat the band but I stood my ground."

"You did just fine, Gramps." Libby shot Jax a look of gratitude as he helped Cleve up the stairs. "It all worked out."

"Won't she be surprised when she gets home and sees I was right all along?" Cleve almost preened at the thought. "She's smart as a whip but there's no flies on me. If you know what I mean."

"That means you're smart." CeeCee offered the old fellow an adorable grin. "You told me that and I believe it, Gramps."

Cleve's smile grew. He took a seat. For the moment, he was happy. Satisfied. But when Jax glanced back at Libby, he read the emotions there.

She knew it wouldn't last. She understood. But how could one woman handle an elderly, sometimes contentious, dementia patient and run an apple orchard at harvest time? With a little girl who loved to run around?

She couldn't.

But she could with his help, and that made it a no-brainer. As long as he could keep his distance.

"Can you say grace, Mr. Jax? Please?"

He froze in place, wondering how to reply.

Libby laid one hand on Cleve's and one on his, and gave a soft blessing. A sweet note of thanks. Then she looked up and met his gaze. Held that look longer than she needed to.

She saw him.

The real him.

He sensed it in her eyes, in her touch, in the prayer. Somehow she glimpsed the soldier behind the civilian facade. The soul-fulness in her gaze reached out to him.

His heart sped up even though it shouldn't. Even though it couldn't.

She held his gaze one beat longer, then smiled.

When she did that, he realized something else. She might be helping him as much as he helped her.

And that wasn't a thought he dared to contemplate.

Chapter Four

"The town won't approve a building permit to replace the barn until they have a plan in front of them," Jax told her the next morning. He tipped his army cap to block the angle of the morning sun as they waited for CeeCee's bus. "I didn't know what you had in mind, because there are several ways to go. We should sit down and talk about it. Get a plan drawn up."

Should she? Libby wondered as CeeCee's bus pulled to a stop in front of them. She kissed CeeCee goodbye and waved until the bus was up the road while she considered the question.

Did it make sense to rebuild the barn if she was going to sell the orchard?

It didn't. Yet it felt wrong not to, as if she was shrugging off part of her family's past. It couldn't be built in time for the current harvest, so what was the point? "I need to really think about this," she told him. "There are multiple issues and we're in a time crunch. I'm in danger of having the Galas overripen, and no place to put them. I asked the Bakers if they wanted to buy them wholesale and market them with theirs, but it's a bumper crop year and they're overloaded. Who would ever think a great harvest was a bad thing?"

"A bumper crop year is perfect for cider production," he noted.

"Gramps was the only one who could get the press to work," she told him. "And the press was in the small barn that no longer exists. When I was a little girl they would buy tons of apples from the other farms to make cider. It was amazing to see. Now most of the apples are produced by the major fruit producers and Gramps stopped pressing cider when it became too difficult to find enough affordable apples. Did you know that our state exports over thirty percent of the apple crop now?"

He hesitated momentarily. "That bothers you?"

She answered as she moved toward the house. "No. It's smart marketing. There's only so much that can be used in one area or even one country. While that drives up the retail prices, it doesn't have the same effect on wholesale prices. People expect us to be lower priced without the middleman but it's a narrow profit margin."

Jax didn't hide his surprise quickly enough and she frowned. "You didn't think I knew about margins and break-even levels and median production, did you?"

He made a face. "Busted."

"I have a bachelor's degree in supply-side logistics and merchandising, but when I got my degree I realized that I didn't care as much about shuffling goods as I did about the presentation of goods. The final package. But one feeds the other, I guess."

"The producer cares about one and the retailer rules the other."

"Exactly." She paused by the door and faced the now-empty barn site before addressing him again. "I want to take a couple of days to figure things out. About the barns, the rebuilding, the deductibles, what makes sense in the long run. I'm not fooling myself about Gramps's condition." She lifted her gaze to his. "I don't know if it makes sense to put all that money into this property and then walk away. And if I *don't* do it, I'm putting another nail in the farm's coffin by inaction, which will limit my choices even further."

He started to speak but paused when she held up a hand. "Give me three days. I'll pray. I'll sound it out with a few others around town and gather some advice. I'm always better when I have the facts surrounding me."

"Fair enough." He motioned toward the

orchard. "I've got some bins being dropped off. We'll get the early apples off the trees this week. I rented some cold storage space just outside town."

She frowned. "That's pricey."

"The insurance had a clause for rental facilities as needed. It wasn't a generous amount, but it will cover a couple of weeks. Enough to buy you a little time."

He'd seen a need and developed a plan, which made him seem even more ideal because he'd not only saved her time, he might have saved the early apples. "That's perfect."

He was carrying a laptop bag over his shoulder. He motioned to it. "Can I take a spot on the back porch and run some figures? If you have Wi-Fi, that is."

"We do and yes. Unless you'd be more comfortable inside?"

He headed for the shaded porch. "Too nice a day. When I was a kid, a day like this was called Washington Perfect. It got to be a saying with my brothers when something went right. We'd look at each other and say, 'Washington Perfect.'"

"How many brothers do you have?" she asked, but the moment she did, he went quiet. Then he answered normally.

"Two. One older, one younger."

She was going to ask if they lived locally, but he was already rounding the corner of the house. Just as well. She didn't need to know personal stuff about him. Nor him about her. She was okay keeping her marriage to Keith to herself.

You're afraid he'll think you were stupid.

She swallowed hard as she climbed the short flight of stairs to the kitchen.

Every time she looked back on the past seven years, she felt stupid. A four-year college degree that she'd barely used, a horrific mistake in her choice of husbands and letting things go long enough to end up homeless. A smart woman would never put an innocent child in those conditions.

"There's my girl!" Joy heightened Gramps's voice when he saw her come through the door. "Come to visit, have you? I'll get Mother. We can set a spell. Okay?"

She couldn't squash his hope and re-explain their circumstances, how she was living with him and that he had a great-granddaughter he recognized some days and not others. "I'd like that, but first I'm going to take care of these dishes, okay?"

"She left them to sit there?" He stared into the kitchen, frowning, because Grandma had always taken pride in a clean kitchen and a job well-done. Libby saw the moment realization hit him. His face dimmed. His eyes lost their sparkle. He didn't say a word. He simply shuffled away to his chair in the front room. He sat and studied the room around him, his eyes darting from this to that.

He was trying to memorize it, she realized.

He was studying things to commit them to memory. Within minutes he would forget again, and these brief moments when he tried to regain a hold on reality hurt the most.

Oblivion came with an air of peace. Realization brought nothing but frustration to a beloved man, but how could she justify hoping for oblivion when he was striving to maintain what little mental capacity remained?

"Keep things as structured and as much the same as you can," the doctor had advised, and she'd been trying to do that, but life had been messing that up lately.

A soft tune came through the open window. Jax whistling "Don't Sit Under the Apple Tree" like he'd done the other day.

Gramps's song.

She took a glass of tea in to Gramps. He greeted her as if she was a waitress in a diner, and when he was settled, she decided she didn't need anyone's advice about the barn.

She was savvy enough to know that easing an old man's last months was worth the cost of a mortgage to pay the balance on the barn. With land prices at record-high levels, she should recoup the investment when she sold the farm eventually. She'd stop by the local bank and get things in motion. They'd want a plan, too, most likely.

She used the back door to access the small porch facing northwest. Jax looked up immediately. The warmth in his expression made her heart stutter again.

She reined in her reaction, then indicated the sloping hills and rugged Cascades beyond them. The arid mountains were brown and bare in spots, a stunning difference to the lush valley below. "We don't do much sitting out here during the cold months."

"Or the front porch, either, I expect, if we get a whip wind."

"And yet we get enough pleasant weather to make a porch seem like something to come home to, don't we?" She crossed to the open post, gazed out, then turned her attention back to him. "I know I said I'd wait, but I decided I want to replace the barn. How do we pick plans to present to the board? Do I need to hire an architect?"

He motioned her closer. "I was just looking at some pole barn packages. You can go old-school with lumber and we can build a wooden barn, but the new pole barns are beautiful and cost-efficient." He'd pulled up a web page of an appealing barn with overhangs on two sides. "I thought the porch covers would be good for outdoor displays. Protection from sun and rain. This model is lower and tighter with no wasted space and you could have a cooler big enough for the small forklift to bring bins in and out."

"It's beautiful."

He nodded. "They've come a long way with these. You could go bigger, but I don't think you need to. Room to store things in the back, room for a produce-type store up front and plenty of refrigerated space."

"How do we get plans and how do we present them to the building inspector?"

"The plans are as easy as pressing a button," he told her. "Do you have a printer?"

"In the front room, yes."

"Wi-Fi enabled?"

She rolled her eyes. "It's supposed to be but isn't, so I keep a cable attached."

He stood, laptop in hand. "Let's print this up and get the ball rolling."

She stepped back.

He didn't want her to, because having her look over his shoulder—her long hair brushing his cheek as she leaned closer to check out the barn's stats—was too good to resist.

He was drawn to her. No denying that.

Her pretty hair smelled of apples and spice. Did she do that purposely, because of the season? Or did she just like the shampoo?

He wanted to know that and so much more, which meant he needed to put the brakes on. Steer clear. Trouble was, he didn't want to. Just as he was thinking those dangerous thoughts, three cars rolled into the driveway. An unlikely looking crew of people piled out. Gert Johnson spotted them and came forward the way she always moved when she wasn't driving a bus. Quickly. "We're here to help, Libby." She motioned to the six local bus drivers gathering around her. "You point us in the right direction and we'll get things going because when Gert Johnson says she'll do somethin', she does it, and the same goes for this motley crew."

"I'll find the printer," he told Libby once he greeted the newcomers. "Then I'll take folks into the orchard and we'll get going on those Galas. How long have you got?" he asked the group, and Slim Viney spoke up first.

"We've got afternoon bus runs at two forty, so we have to leave here by two fifteen to get back in time. And we'll be doing this every day until the job's done. That's what folks do in Golden Grove." He aimed a significant look in Libby's direction. "They shore each other up when the chips are down."

"Sure do!" said Dora Donaldson, a stout but lively woman who helped run the church calendar for Golden Grove's oldest church. Her great-grandfather had been one of the first settlers this side of Quincy, and he'd worked side by side with Jax's great-grandfather a long time ago. Jax used his middle name as a surname here. If he uttered the name Ingerson, his relationship to CVF would be instantly known. Loved by some, hated by a few, his family had invested time and money to grow their business over four generations. He wasn't one bit ashamed of that. He simply wanted to fly under the radar for a while.

His conscience scoffed as he went inside to hook up his laptop.

Three years and counting. That's a long penance by anyone's standards.

Would it ever be long enough when four of his men drew a death sentence that day? A dull throbbing began to take root at his temples. A throbbing that could explode into a massive headache.

Sit. Breathe. Do the relaxation techniques you've been taught. You can interrupt this cycle.

But he had no time to sit and do the breathing exercises to relax the muscles that clenched when memories came flooding back. He needed to get the barn plans printed and get into that orchard. He'd offered his help. Painful head or not, he'd made a promise. Now he had to keep it.

He frowned, crossed to the slim desk in the narrow hallway, hooked the laptop to the printer, printed a double set of plans, then checked on Cleve.

The old man had dozed off in his chair. His food was untouched. Jax debated leaving it there or taking it back to the kitchen. In the end, he left it. Cleve might eat when he woke up or might forget to eat at all, another disease conundrum. He started to head out, but a group of photos on the nearby wall caught his eye. He moved closer.

A middle-aged couple snuggled a little

girl who looked a lot like CeeCee. Bright blue eyes laughed into the camera while a younger Cleve's salt-and-pepper hair lay against the little girl's golden curls. His wife seemed amused and delighted by something. Their antics, maybe? And this picture was flanked by a half-dozen other pics of Libby at various ages. The grandparents' love for her was obvious. He also noted a conspicuous lack of parents in the photos.

"Them were good times for the most part."

Cleve's voice startled him.

The printer clicked off right then, too.

The old fellow looked that way, frowned and lifted his plate of food. "Mother never lets me eat out here, she must be gettin' daft in her old age." He giggled as if he was getting away with something and began taking small bites of food. "She said, 'Cleveland O'Laughlin, we've got a child to raise and we need to set a good example.'"

"She meant Libby, I expect?"

The old man frowned. "Who?"

Jax saw no sense in riling the old fellow up so he changed the subject. "How's your breakfast?"

"Good enough. Could use more salt."

Libby came in just then, Gert came along with her. When she spotted Libby's grandfather, she crossed the room and gave the old fellow a quick hug. "Cleve, it's me, Gert Johnson. I live over on East Third Street, remember?"

"I don't remember much, but I do recall that pretty face and a white wedding gown when you and B.J. Johnson got married a ways back."

"Do tell." She crouched low and smiled at him. "That was a fine wedding, wasn't it?"

"It was." He nodded, then tried to angle a bite of scrambled egg onto a piece of toast. One hand missed the other and the egg fell with a light *plop* onto the plate. "I was just tellin' Mother that we haven't seen you folks in a while. Got any kids yet?"

Libby started to interrupt, but Gert rose

to the challenge nicely. "Four, and they are my pride and joy. I'm just stoppin' in with some of my bus drivin' friends to do some apple pickin' for you, so if you see any of us wanderin' round, we're supposed to be here. Okay?"

"It's picking time?" He peered toward the window as if checking the leaves and the weather for confirmation.

"It sure is," she told him, "and we've got the best crew on board to help Libby while you folks put things to rights."

"Libby." He frowned, stared at Gert, then Jax and then Libby. "I don't know a Libby. My wife's name is Carolyn. She'll be out here soon, I expect, especially when she sees me eating in the living room."

Unremembered. Unappreciated. Misunderstood.

Jax remembered the drill like it was yesterday, not a dozen years before. How his brothers shied away from Grandma Molly's sharp tongue and wild ramblings because it hurt to be forgotten. It hurt to be overlooked by someone who loved you enough to raise you to be fine young men. He looked at Libby.

She'd wiped the frown from her face and moved forward. "I think Grandma would approve. She gave me her permission to let you eat out here when CeeCee and I moved in last year. She wanted you happy and healthy, Gramps."

He frowned, then slapped a hand to the chair arm. "Oh, Libby! Yep, I recall a Libby now, a little girl, real pretty curls and we had to straighten her teeth. Cost a fair penny, too, but in for a penny, in for a pound, I like to say."

"And very pretty teeth they are," quipped Jax. He smiled at Libby to ease the moment, then raised the sheaf of papers in his hand. "I'm going to put a set of these in the truck, then I'll take the pickers into the orchard. We'll start filling sacks and bins. I saw a pile of apple sacks on the back porch." Apple sacks were strong canvas bags draped around the neck, leaving both hands free to pick fruit.

"I washed the dust out of them over the weekend, so they were spared the onslaught of the wind," Libby told him. "There's about fifteen there. Take what you need."

"Will do." He reached over and touched Cleve on the shoulder. "I'll be picking apples today, too. If you want to take a walk or give us a hand with the Galas, I'd be happy to have you by my side."

"I'm fast," Cleve warned him, and he puffed up his chest when he said it. "Folks couldn't believe how fast I was when it came to apples, but I don't let anything keep me down. Persistence runs in my family, you know."

"I'm sure it does." Jax stepped back.

Libby took Cleve's empty plate and moved back, too.

She didn't look pained by the old man's pendulum swings of behavior and memory. She took the plate to the kitchen quietly, then rinsed it under a stream of water. He followed to use the side door but paused when he noticed three new crayon drawings of doglike creatures on the refrigerator. "CeeCee's been planning her campaign, I see."

"Oh, she has." Libby sent the new dog images a bemused look. "She wants a dog in the worst way, so her renditions of Dreamer keep appearing throughout the house. There was even one on the upstairs bathroom mirror this morning."

"I hear persistence runs in the family," he teased.

"And then some," Libby replied. "But I can barely stay afloat with what I've got going now. How do I add a dog into the mix?" She shrugged. "Maybe next year. I need to know where I'll be before I can commit to something that's going to be around for a dozen years or more. Do you have a dog?" she asked. For some reason, the question caught him off guard. He almost stuttered his reply.

"I did. Now I don't."

She noticed the pain in his voice. He saw the recognition in her face. "It's hard to say goodbye, isn't it?"

He'd never gotten a chance to say goodbye. Flint had died four weeks before he'd come home, killed by a hit-and-run driver.

His friends gone because of a mechanical mistake.

His dog gone when a careless driver had left him lying in a ditch along Route 2. He walked toward the back door. "I'm going to stow these, put my laptop away, then get to work." Thoughts of Flint and the war put a vise grip on his temples.

He stowed the computer and the barn plans, grabbed a stack of bags and gave one to each bus driver. While the earnest pickers began bringing in what might be Cleve O'Laughlin's final harvest, he piled apple crates onto his truck, then unloaded them in strategic locations along the straight, trimmed rows of the old-style orchard.

He'd made it through these last few years by keeping busy, holding thoughts at bay.

As long as he was moving, he could make it through the days because if he stayed busy enough, there wasn't time to consider the problems that plagued him at night.

The doctor had prescribed sleeping pills.

Jax refused to take them because being kept asleep artificially was almost as scary as being unable to sleep. What if the meds never wore off and he just stayed asleep forever?

He shoved the thoughts aside, dropped off the crates, then joined the pickers, doing a job he'd been raised to do from the time he could walk. To pick Washington Perfect apples, like everyone in his family before him. For today it would be enough if the pain would just stop.

Chapter Five

"I'm sorry, Libby." Sylvia Drummond, the local bank officer, met with Libby the next day. She sounded apologetic, but sympathy wasn't going to keep things afloat on the farm. "I've run the numbers on your application for the mortgage and they don't work. The bank has to turn down your request because there isn't enough sustainable income to make it a worthy risk. If you were working, it would be different, but you're not."

How did one work while caring for a sick relative? Or did people expect her to shut Gramps in a home and walk away? Doing that would solve several problems. She could work. The mortgage would be approved. And Gramps would be cared for every single day with no worry on her part except that the person who raised her would suffer.

"I'll go back to work once Gramps gets either too sick for me to care for at home, or—" she had to swallow hard at this part "—when he's gone. But for now it's impossible to hold down a job and care for Gramps and the farm. And there's clearly no money for before-and after-school care unless I'm working, and if I'm working, I can't take care of Gramps."

"A catch-22, for sure," the bank officer agreed. "I've known your grandparents since I was a kid. Your grandma had such a giving heart. Cleve, too, although he's always had a stubborn streak."

A streak that deepened with his illness.

"Unfortunately a decision like this is out of my hands when the numbers are this far off, Libby. Will insurance money cover most of the barn? Can you scale back the building size to fit the insurance payout?"

"The plans *are* downsized," she explained, and she held out the online pictures of the proposed barn. "Not an inch of wasted space, and it's a pole barn, so we're saving there, too, but construction isn't cheap and the insurance will only cover about a third of the cost."

Sylvia's mouth thinned. "So the barn would eat up every penny of the insurance payout and the loan."

"Yes."

"And it wouldn't be ready in time for this year's crop sales in any case."

Libby's chest tightened further. "Correct."

Sylvia sighed softly. "I know that CVF has been buying land in your area. Everyone is aware of it, and while we'll all miss our roadside stands, have you considered offering them the orchard lands? I know CVF is huge, but they're good land stewards and everyone who borders their orchards is pleased to have them as a neighbor. Would it be in your best interest to sell them the land and ask if you can occupy the house temporarily? Or maybe have the house acreage legally separated from the orchards and sell just the farmland. That would leave the house free and clear," she continued. "And money in the bank from the sale. Would Cleve even have to know that the orchard changed hands? That could get you by until…"

Sylvia meant well, and in some ways it made perfect sense, but her proposal meant that Libby and CeeCee had to use lies and deceit to cover up the land sale. If Gramps found out accidentally, he would be crushed.

She'd be following Grandma's request in deed, but not in spirit, and she'd be doing it dishonestly. "I can't lie to him." She stood, effectively ending the discussion. "He helped raise me. He taught me everything I know about orcharding, and these sixty acres have been in the family for generations. My great-great-grandfather was given irrigation rights in the early part of the twentieth century and we've planted and replanted this land ever since. Thank you." Even though the bank's position put her in a severe money crunch, she refused to forget her manners. "I understand the numbers behind your decision, but I want to thank you for considering me."

She shook Sylvia's hand and left the bank with her chin held high. It didn't matter that she choked back tears once she stood on the sidewalk.

She'd held it together inside.

Grandma had always taught her to have a plan B. She'd lost her ability to arrange a secondary plan when her marriage fell apart. Once she saw Keith's true colors, she realized that keeping CeeCee and herself safe had to be first on her agenda. He'd definitely done her a favor by walking out.

As she drove home, she counted her blessings. She had CeeCee, her beloved child. She had this time with Gramps, something to cherish in the years to come. She had a house with a solid roof. And as she pulled into the farm driveway and spotted Jax Mc-Claren's white truck, a part of her wanted to count his friendship as a blessing.

But she couldn't.

Nice handyman that he was, he was doing them a service as a kindness, nothing more. But when the truck came her way, he slowed it down long enough to tip his hat and smile in her direction as he pulled up to another stack of apple bins.

Her heart beat faster.

She ordered it to stop.

It didn't listen, and when she climbed out of the patched-up O'Laughlin farm truck, she was determined to walk straight into that house and get on with her day.

"Need help with anything?" he asked, his voice full of kindness.

She started to wave him off, then paused. "Are you all right?"

"Fine, thanks."

He wasn't, though. He winced slightly as she stepped closer. "You don't look fine."

"Well, gee. Thank you." He gave her a roguish grin to lighten the moment. "Just what every fellow wants to hear. How'd things go in town?"

"They didn't. I don't have enough income to secure the loan and there's no way I can work off the farm and be away from Gramps, so we might have to table the barn notion. With the insurance shortfall, and no way to fund the balance, it's a no-go."

He looked at her, then the barn spot, then her again. "Creative financing is one of my specialties."

"We need to go beyond *creative* in this case," she told him.

"I know some private investors who understand the fruit market. A bank has overseers to report to. A private investor doesn't. The fruit on those trees is a hanging gold mine, but we need to get it into the consumers' hands. Money isn't our conundrum."

She made a face because she was pretty sure that finances were a huge problem.

"We need to establish a selling spot. That's the only thing holding us back."

"Tents?"

He didn't laugh at her. In fact, the idea seemed to intrigue him. "I might be able to come up with one. One of those big ones. Not ideal, but better than nothing, right?"

It would be different, but it would give her the necessary cover she needed. There wouldn't be much road appeal, but for this season, it might work. "That would be a help."

"I'll make a couple of calls."

"Can I get you something for that headache you're pretending not to have?"

He got a funny look on his face, then shook his head. "It's gone, actually. I thought it was going to be a killer afternoon, but it's gone."

"Good. And if I haven't thanked you enough, Jax, let me say it again. There's no way I could be getting all this done without your help. You've taken a huge load of stress off my shoulders. I'm not sure how you just happened along at the right time, but you did. And I'm so grateful." She took his hand. A simple gesture of sincerity, but then she didn't want to let go of his hand. Let go of him.

"My pleasure, ma'am."

Oh, that smile. The cowboy tone. That look when he touched a finger to that army cap. She could get used to that look. She didn't dare consider it…

And yet she couldn't help thinking about it as she went inside.

"That you, Carolyn?" Gramps called out as she slung her purse over a kitchen hook. "I was bringing my clothes out for a washin'. You always liked to do washing on Mondays, didn't you?" And there was Gramps, in shorts and a T-shirt, lugging a basket of clean laundry in his arms.

"It's Libby, Gramps, but I'll be happy to take care of that for you. Where's Mortie?"

The nurse came out of Gramps's bedroom

just then, carrying a medicine container. "Libby, you're back. I was just checking on Cleve's meds for him and—" She sized up the laundry basket, Gramps's clothing and the situation quickly. "But I'll let you get that laundry taken care of first. Then we'll talk. Cleve, it's not cold out, but it's not shorts-wearing weather, either. If you want to help that nice young man with the apples, you're going to need to put something warmer on."

He handed Libby the basket and studied the small calendar on the living room table. "It says September."

Libby nodded.

"It is September, Cleve," Mortie assured him. "Time for harvest."

"Then we better do what they did in the Bible, don't you think? Get those laborers on board. Though they only paid a penny for a day's work in that scripture. I expect we'll have to go a little higher." He grinned.

"We're setting up for the harvest right now, Gramps."

He rubbed gleeful hands together. "This is where I'm at my best. Old-fashioned hard work. And I don't need a cent of pay because those apple sales are my money in the bank every year."

Mortie understood their circumstances. Gramps didn't.

The home health nurse reached a hand out to his arm. "Well, let's get some proper picking clothes for you, all right?"

"Don't know what I was thinkin'!" He followed her like a happy pup and when he emerged a few moments later, he was wearing sweatpants and a long-sleeved pullover. "Now I'm ready."

"I'm on my way out, so I'll see you over to where that nice young man is getting things organized." Mortie grabbed her bag and the light sweater she'd laid along the back of the couch.

"Sounds good."

Jax spotted them coming out the door. He crossed the driveway quickly and motioned to the truck. "Cleve, I'm just heading out to set bins and I've got a picking bag with your name on it. Want to ride along?"

"Don't mind if I do. Who are you?" he asked bluntly. "I don't know you, do I?"

"Jax." He stuck out a hand and gave Gramps that sweet smile. "I've hired on for the season, sir."

"I hope you brought a passel of friends because we've got our work cut out for us. We'll fill that barn so full to burstin' that we'll have a year's supply of money in the bank by November. And then some," he boasted.

"Sounds like a plan." Jax directed him to the truck and opened the door for him. Once Gramps had climbed in, Jax turned. He gave the women a quiet thumbs-up. And when he rounded the truck, he spoke softly, so Gramps wouldn't overhear. "You gals do what you need to do. I've got this."

He offered a respite.

Libby hadn't realized how desperately she needed a break until it was offered.

She smiled her thanks and turned toward Mortie. "You needed to see me."

"I do, and it's not easy, is it? Your grandpa's got a heart of gold but he's developing the impish nature of a preschooler in some ways. This might be our most dangerous time yet because his trips to reality are growing scarce."

"Is it normal to go downhill this fast?" Libby asked, and Mortie shrugged.

"It's not all that fast, sweet thing. It's been accumulating for years. We're just now seeing the results of the buildup."

"Like when a slow-running drain finally gets fully clogged."

"Just like that. And this could go on for a long time or a relatively short time, there's no way of knowing." Mortie put an arm around Libby's shoulders. "I'm going to recommend an increase in care time. His insurance will cover it and you need it. The problem is, if he gets contentious, the health care workers don't always stay. We don't pay them enough to be yelled at or scolded or ridiculed, and those are common enough occurrences with dementia."

Libby knew that firsthand. "Gramps has gone off on me a few times lately."

"And that's not one bit fun, is it?" Mortie asked softly. "To have our mistakes or missteps thrown up at us long after we've moved on. Another sorrow of this wretched disease, but here's what I'm saying to you." She turned and faced Libby fully. "This is not your grandpa talking, even if it sounds, looks and feels like it is. It's like when an internet connection goes weak and all you get is that spinning little circle taking you absolutely nowhere."

"Buffering is such a pain," Libby agreed.

"That's what his brain is doing when he goes off like that. It's buffering, searching for information, for memories, and usually failing. Don't think of it as being aimed at you, even when it sounds that way. Think of it as being plain old stuck. And move on."

She gave Mortie a quick hug. "I'll keep

that in mind. And thanks for recommending more help, Mortie. I sure could use it."

"Well, it's time," Mortie replied. "I'll see you soon, but if you need me, call me. Or call the doctor's office and they'll get hold of me right quick. If we approach this as a team, we're all better for it."

"I will. And, Mortie, thank you for being here. I don't know what I'd do without you."

Mortie's compassion warmed her smile. "That's what friends and neighbors are for, Libby. To shore one another up as needed because there but for the grace of God go I. And that can be said for every one of us." She climbed into her car, started it up and did a K-turn. "I'll give you a call, okay?"

"Yes."

She watched Mortie leave. Gramps was safe with Jax for a while and she had time to get something done. What she really wanted was to go to the front porch, curl up on the glider and read a book.

But nobody in the apple business had time to read books in the fall, so she shelved that idea until January, took care of some things inside and pushed aside her worries about money. If Jax could find a tent, two weeks of fruit sales would bridge her current gap.

But how would a tent hold up in a storm? What if this was an ongoing weather trend?

She couldn't change the weather. But she could put the whole thing squarely where it belonged, in God's hands. He'd gotten her this far. One way or another He'd get her through what could be Gramps's final harvest.

Chapter Six

Glenn Moyer stopped by the next morning to offer the use of the old barn to the east, the one CeeCee had drawn.

Libby had to fight back tears when he made the offer. "But you sold the land, Mr. Moyer. That's what Gramps said."

"I did. But I kept the plot with the barn in case Tug wanted to use it. CVF had no use for it, and that single acre didn't make much of a difference in the sale price, so keeping it made sense. It hasn't been used in a bunch of years, but the fruit cooler worked fine the last time we turned it on." The middle-aged farmer made a sour face.

"It's not pretty, but it gives you an option for marketing your fruit until you can re-build. I'd help clean it up but Tug's got his hands full with two kids and no wife, so Darla and I are over there all the time."

Glenn's daughter-in-law had passed away three years ago, leaving their son Tug with two kids and a full-time job with the sheriff's department. "He's blessed to have your help, Glenn. Thank you." She hugged him, then drew back, embarrassed. "I'm sorry, it's been a crazy few days and I'm more emotional than normal. But you deserved that hug."

The hug made him laugh. Or her reaction. Maybe both. "I'll take it in any case," he told her, grinning. "And if you need help minding the stand, let me know. There are a couple of local gals who know the value of hard work, which means they don't stand around staring at their phones for fourteen dollars an hour. They're in college now, but I expect available enough to spell you now and again. I'll text you their names and numbers."

Fourteen dollars an hour.

She pretended that sounded like a good option even though there was no money to pay anyone anything at the moment. "Thank you so much."

"We were real sorry to hear about what happened over here," he added as he moved toward his truck. "You folks didn't deserve this, but life isn't about deserving, is it? It's about facing the day and getting on with things."

A Western code, something she didn't understand as a child. She understood it now as a single mom with an ill grandparent. Worrying did no good. But mustering up, getting things done, that was what got folks through. And the strong faith she'd shrugged off as a younger woman?

That was her mainstay now.

True to their word, the seven bus drivers came by after their morning runs, and when Gert realized that the borrowed barn wasn't ready for displaying apples, she organized a team to clean it out, with a promise that they could open the doors in time to welcome the late-September influx of weekend shoppers and leaf peepers.

They scrubbed the Moyers' old fruit cooler, and when they hooked up the electricity, the lights came on and the cooler got cold, two simple but vital things for fruit sales and storage.

By the end of the week they'd harvested the first two apple varieties and the popular Italian plums, now sweet and succulent. The bulk of the apples would ripen in October, but for now they had something to sell. But how could she sell apples a quarter mile up the road with the work to be done here and taking care of Gramps?

The now-familiar white pickup truck rolled into the driveway as she and CeeCee waited for the bus that morning. CeeCee dashed forward once Jax parked the truck. "Mr. Jax! Wait till you see this!" She yanked her backpack off. It tumbled to the ground. Then she grabbed a folded-up paper from the first zippered compartment. "I put it in here so I wouldn't forget where it was," she told him as she handed it over. "It's Dreamer with you. Can you tell? I even put your hat on you, so you wouldn't get the sun in your eyes while you played with him. And your name, too, see? Only Mommy had to tell me how to spell it, and it wasn't one bit hard!"

Jax gave a soft whistle of appreciation. "You drew this? For me?"

CeeCee beamed. She nodded quickly, like she couldn't wait to confirm the gesture. "I knew you liked dogs because every time I talk about Dreamer, you listen, and if you didn't like dogs, you wouldn't even really listen to me, right?"

Guilt shot through Libby.

Was she guilty of brushing off CeeCee's dreams about a dog because she knew it wasn't possible right now? Jax squatted to CeeCee's level, and he looked her square in the eye. "I will treasure this, CeeCee. I'll put it on my refrigerator—"

CeeCee's eyes went wide because she knew what an honor it was to have your work on someone's refrigerator.

"And every morning and evening I'll see it and remember that my friend Cecelia thought enough of me to make me a beautiful picture." The rumble of the oncoming bus drew his gaze up. "Your chariot arrives, m'lady."

CeeCee giggled, started to grab her backpack, but then hugged Jax instead. "Thank you, Mr. Jax. For helping us. And for being my good, good friend!"

It wasn't CeeCee's spontaneity or words that got Libby choked up.

It was Jax's face, as if this wasn't just a cute little kid hug. It was something much, much more. He didn't just accept the hug.

He leaned down, gathered CeeCee into his arms and walked her to the bus. "Special delivery," he announced as Gert opened the door.

She laughed.

So did the kids on the bus, and CeeCee climbed those steps with such an air of confidence that Libby got emotional.

He came back her way and waved the bus off with her. "That's some kid you've got, ma'am."

"She's pretty cute, all right. And she's excited about helping out at the barn and selling apples, but I'm not sure how to keep an eye on Gramps with the barn so far away. We were able to sell last year's harvest out of our own barn so I was close by. And we had health aides in and out every day for Grandma. This quarter-mile distance makes a big difference."

He glanced up the road, then back at the house. "When is Cleve's best time usually?"

"Mornings in general, but it's more sporadic now. We don't really have a best time anymore. Just the occasional good moments."

"That's what I've been seeing with him,

too." He surveyed the house and orchard, and the far-off barn with a quick look. "How about if you have him with you for the mornings, then he comes back here for the afternoons? It's not perfect, but if I'm working here, I can set up a camera app in the living room and keep an eye on him if I'm in the orchard. The crew from the bus garage is keeping us on our toes, and I found a couple of fellows looking for work in town, so I hired them beginning tomorrow. We've got to get the next apples picked and into storage before the weather turns."

"I can't pay them." Libby hated admitting that out loud. "There's no money until we start selling apples. If I'd been able to work this last year, we'd be fine, but that wasn't possible with Grandma's illness and now Gramps. His monthly check barely covers the few bills they have and I had to use his savings for a midsummer tractor repair and to pay for the chemicals we needed. If ever I was looking for some divine intervention on what to do, it's now. The farm can't sustain itself with no income and I've got none until the first fruits sell."

She should be hopeless. Or look hopeless, because she was faced with a host of problems. Except she wasn't despairing. Resigned, yes. Desperate? No. And for just a moment he wanted some of whatever it was that made her that way. Something to fall back on. He'd had that faith platform a long time ago, but the cornerstones he'd stood on all seemed to crumble in the Iraqi desert. He swallowed hard and focused on here and now. "First off, the barn is no worry, and the board approval meeting is tomorrow night. If we have someone sit with Cleve, can I attend the meeting with you? Not because I doubt your capabilities," he clarified when she lifted a brow. "The board is used to seeing me. I've worked on a number of projects in town the past few years."

"So you're a contractor."

He wouldn't lie to her. "More of a handyman, but when it comes to hammers and nails and board feet, I'm your go-to man."

"So your wages for all of this work go into the pricing for the barn, right? Then I pay you out of the insurance money?"

He wouldn't need to be paid.

He knew that. She didn't. And if he raised the point, she'd start asking questions about who he was and where the money came from. Eventually it would come to light that the CVF Heritage Foundation was footing the bill for any extras, but she didn't need to know that right now. "It all comes out as a wash in the end. We can go over figures sometime soon."

"I do better with figures," she told him. "I don't like surprises and I don't like handing over control."

"Then let's do that now," he told her, but her phone interrupted them. She scanned the display and frowned.

"I've got to take this—it's the health service."

"We can talk later, then." He watched her as she moved away with the phone.

She was up and working when he got there in the mornings, and she was still working with CeeCee on homework or other duties when he left at night. And in between she oversaw Cleve's well-being, while running the farm.

Yet she seemed ashamed that she hadn't been able to hold down a full-time job while doing all that.

He took his truck into the orchard, but before he set out new bins, he put in a call to his father. "Hey, Dad. It's me."

Richard Ingerson laughed. "The phone number was a clue. How are you doing? Aunt Connie wanted to drive over there last week, but I talked her out of it when I heard you were on a new project."

Aunt Connie had a big heart and a take-charge attitude. She loved him and his brothers, but she wasn't subtle. And he'd avoided her for the last year and a half, which meant he'd avoided most family functions. His father, on the other hand, let him know he was concerned on a regular basis, but with such love that Jax couldn't be upset about it. "It's a project that involves you, actually."

"Me?"

"Central Valley Fruit."

"I'm listening."

Jax explained the history, the location and the situation. "I know you've put in an offer on the farm and that Cleve rejected it."

His father sighed. "Legal approached him first. Then we had Ken offer a contract. In return, the old man offered to show him to the door with a vintage bent-barrel shotgun."

Cleve had a gun?

Firearms and dementia or PTSD or any kind of mental disorder didn't go well together. Making sure the gun went into hiding would be first on Jax's new to-do list.

"He didn't get the gun, but then the representative didn't hang around to push his luck, either."

"The farm's being run by his granddaughter," Jax explained. "She's in a really rough spot financially, but doesn't want to sell the farm out from under him. He's dying, Dad."

"Jackson." His father's voice went deep. "You've had enough on your plate these past few years, haven't you? Maybe this isn't the best project for you to take on. Maybe you should—"

Jax cut him off before his father could finish. "Insulate myself from life? Like I've been doing? Except I can't this time. This old man, and Libby—"

"Libby?"

"His granddaughter, the woman running things. They had a dream and we can't wreck that. But she's literally out of money."

"The foundation already approved the extra rebuilding costs, didn't it?"

"Yes. But what they really need is customers. Business. I want them to feel like this harvest is the most successful one ever, and right now she'll be selling out of a roughed-up barn up the road. No signage. No advertising. Nothing to bring people this way. But there's no time or money to change things."

"If a couple of old friends happen to stop by and help you get the barn in order…"

"I love it when friends and family get together," he replied in kind, which was funny because he'd purposely avoided friends and family for much of the last three years, mostly because they'd ask how he was doing, and the last thing he wanted to talk about was how he was doing. It was easier to just stay out of sight.

"I'll have people there in an hour. Call in an order to Ag Supply in Quincy and I'll have your cousins pick it up on the way. And, Jax?"

"Yeah?"

"I'm glad you brought this to our attention. Your great-grandfather knew this man's father, and he respected him. If this is his final harvest, we'll make sure it's a great one."

"Thanks, Dad." He hung up the phone, waited until the bus drivers arrived, and once he assigned them areas, he stopped by the house and tapped on the side door. He stepped inside when Libby motioned him in. "Our crew has arrived and I've shown them what to do, but I want to do some cosmetic work on the barn before you open up. Are you okay here?"

"Fine, but I don't know how much you can really do." She'd been working at her laptop. She stood and came his way. "Additional display shelves would be wonderful. We've got an account at the ag store in Quincy, and we could pay it off with the first sales."

"I've got a couple of guys who said they'd stop by and help out." He wasn't lying. He was just simplifying the truth. "I'll have one of them grab some shelving lumber. It's amazing what you can do with focused light and solid shelving."

"Two rules of merchandising," she agreed. "Keep it bright and full, and within easy reach."

He turned to go, but then paused. "Libby, there's another thing that occurred to me today."

"Oh? What was that?"

"Does Cleve own a gun?"

She winced instantly. "Two," she said softly. "And he doesn't have them locked up. I took all the ammunition I could find so they're never loaded. Still, even the thought of him doing something foolish with a gun when he's not in his right mind scares me."

She was right to be scared. If Cleve went off with a gun in hand, authorities would have no way of knowing it wasn't loaded and they'd respond accordingly. "Can you get them to me and I'll make them disappear for the duration?"

"Yes, absolutely." Relief softened the worry line that had formed between her brows. "That's a great idea. I'll gather them while he's sleeping and put them in the back of my truck. You can pick them up from there. And if he goes looking, I'll just say I haven't seen them in a while. He'll be frustrated, but that's better than a possible alternative. I'll give you the ammo, too."

"And I'll put them all in a safe place," he promised. Not at his cabin. He hadn't allowed himself to keep a weapon since coming home, for the very same reasons he was removing Cleve's now. In the midst of a night terror, the last thing a person should have was a gun. "If you need me, just call," he added. He moved toward the door.

So did she.

She smelled of apple-scented dish soap and spiced shampoo. He wanted to lean closer. Breathe in the scent of her. Inspire the smile that seemed to wind its way around his heart.

She motioned beyond him. "I've got to change laundry loads. Gramps's bedding needed a full washing and I have to get the bed remade before he decides to nap there."

"I could keep him busy for a few minutes. Or make the bed," he told her. He'd done plenty of bed making in the service, although you wouldn't know it to see his cabin right now.

"No need," she said. "I'll have it done quickly. Mortie is coming around eleven, then coming back tomorrow to train a home health aide to come each day. That will give me a couple of hours to work in the apples. Unless you need me at the barn?"

The barn was the last place he wanted her today. "No, you can hang here. We'll throw up some shelves and make sure the bins in the cooler won't need a forklift to bring them down."

"Perfect." She smiled up at him.

He smiled back. And he didn't want to stop smiling. She lightened something within him. Her hope persevering through despair. Her calm in a storm. Her strength inspired his desire to be strong again. To be the best he could be. To make him care.

Those pretty blue eyes. Lightly tanned cheeks from working the orchard all summer. Was her skin as soft as it looked? Did he dare find out?

She didn't seem to be in a hurry to break the connection, either, but when his gaze went to her mouth, she stepped back.

It was the right move. If he couldn't trust himself in the grip of a night terror, how could he expect someone else to have faith in him?

That made walking out that door imperative, even if it was the last thing he wanted to do. And right now, to his surprise, it was.

Chapter Seven

She was attracted to the kind, hardworking handyman she knew nothing about. A man who seemed to have an answer for everything. How was that possible?

Yes, she was a woman of faith, and in simplistic terms she could write this off as God's timing. Maybe it was, but Jax's presence, his goodwill and his willingness to pitch in and help weren't normal.

Normal people had jobs to go to every day. Normal people couldn't just take weeks off and help out a neighbor.

He said you could work out pay after the

insurance check comes. Why are you bor-
rowing trouble?

She knew why as she laid out Cleve's
clothes the next morning.

Trouble had found her often enough. Her
parents. Her husband. She hadn't just promised herself she'd be more discerning. She'd
promised God, and great guys didn't just
happen along the two-lane and become a
superhero, did they? And yet, Jax McClaren
had done just that. A text came through just
then. From Jax. I need the morning to finish up in the barn. Can you get the pickers situated when they arrive? I'm going to
have a friend start moving all the apples
over to this barn. Okay?

That saves cooler rent in town, so yes.
Wonderful. Thank your friend for me. I'll
take care of everything here.

A thumbs-up emoji appeared.

The emoji disappointed her. She didn't
want the conversation to end. Was it be-

cause she was smitten? Or lonely? Maybe both, which meant maybe she should reconsider adopting a dog, because lonely women were prone to doing foolish things.

Not her. Not now. Not ever again. No matter how nice his smile was. And it wasn't just nice. When he looked at her, it was absolutely swoon-worthy. Fortunately she'd erected a swoon-resistant wall a long time ago, but when Jax was around, the wall seemed to crumble.

She spotted a produce truck going by midafternoon. Apple crates lined the truck's profile. The truck turned into the barn driveway, and an arrow of expectation shot through her. She'd always loved the sales season on the farm. Working with pickers, with Grandma and Gramps. "This'll all be yours someday, toots," he'd tell her, grinning as he said the words. "Your place. Your farm. Your fruit. O'Laughlin Orchards. Owner/manager, Liberty Creighton."

Growing up, she'd dreamed of having

her own apple stand, her own shop. But then she'd made other choices in college. If she'd stuck with the plan, maybe Gramps wouldn't be in this financial crisis now. If she'd stayed and worked the farm like she'd promised—

"Libby?" Mortie's voice interrupted her thoughts.

She came around the back of the house as her phone signaled a text. Apples have arrived. Need guidance. Are you available?

Mortie just got here, she texted back. I'll be right over.

A young woman was with Mortie, and they both came toward Libby. "Libby, this is Courtney Meyers. She's going to be your new home health aide."

"Welcome." Libby extended her hand. "Your time here is important to us, Courtney, and my granddad isn't always in the best frame of mind. I hope—"

"I lost two great-uncles to Alzheimer's," the younger woman said. "Two kind, funny men who weren't all that kind and funny when their brains stopped working right, so I know the confusion can make people nervous. Or make them snap over little things. I'm new at doing this, but not so new at life."

Libby could appreciate those words better than most, because she'd become an old hand at life's turns and twists at a mighty young age. "Then I'm glad to meet you. Let me take you guys in. Gramps was awake when I came out back, but he may have dozed off now."

"And waste a September day sleepin' when I should be workin'?" Cleve half bellowed the words as he came toward the door. He'd been dressed in the sweatpants and pull-on shirt that worked well inside the house and out, but Gramps had always worn his old bib overalls during picking time.

He must have gone digging for them, because Libby hadn't seen them since the close of harvest last year. He'd found them, though. They were wrinkled and he'd pulled them on backward. One arm was through the metal-clasped suspender. The other suspender was left dangling. "They don't fit like they used to," he complained as the women went through the door. "I told Carolyn I thought I'd dropped some weight, but she's been busy, you know, takin' care of Libby. Shoulda gone and done the shopping myself."

"Cleve, I do not think it's the overalls that are the problem," Mortie declared. She laughed, and to Libby's relief, Gramps laughed, too. "Remember how we said those snaps were getting hard on old fingers? Well, let's see if we can get these pants to fit properly. I know you like wearing them," she continued. She ushered Gramps back inside as she spoke, and sent Libby a quiet look, mouthing, *I've got this.*

Libby took the hint.

Gramps would argue less with Mortie about the overalls, and if Mortie was here for a few hours, she could go up the road to the barn with a clear conscience.

She was halfway there when she realized something was different. Quite different. As she got closer, she slowed the car down, amazed.

The front of the barn gleamed with fresh red paint. Above the doors, someone had painted "O'Laughlin Orchards, Fine Fruits in Season" and the two old windows that faced the road had been replaced with new insulated windows that gleamed in the afternoon sun. The old sliding door had been replaced by two nine-light country-friendly doors with cross-buck bottoms, all trimmed out in the barn-red-and-white motif.

The driveway and parking area had been smoothed. Fresh gray stone led right to the barn, and along the front of the barn stood thick, sturdy display tables. Three for apples, one for plums, one with firewood and kindling and one marked "Just-picked vegetables."

She hadn't grown a single tomato this year. And not one pepper, but this table was plainly marked with a kaleidoscope of veggie tags. Bicolor Sweet Corn. Green Peppers. Red Peppers. Butternut Squash. Sweet Onions. And more.

She parked the old truck in front and stepped down.

Jax hadn't just cleaned up the place. He'd detailed it, giving curb appeal top priority and as she was wrapping her head around that, he appeared at the double doors. "You like?"

Did she like it?

Her eyes started filling with tears.

Jax stopped instantly, hands up, palms out. "Whoa."

His reaction made her laugh back the tears. "What did you expect?" she scolded as she swiped the backs of her hands to her cheeks. "This isn't just throwing up a few shelving units to hold apples."

"We did that, too, and we added some more lighting. And a dividing wall there, so you can run equipment in the back and keep the front clean for sales."

"I can't believe this."

"I didn't do it alone," he went on, as if he'd done nothing big at all. "A couple of buddies pitched in yesterday. It's all surface stuff." He stepped aside as she walked inside. "But it makes it more approachable and noticeable, right?"

"Absolutely." They'd installed three rows of two-tiered shelving inside. And two large old china cabinets stood along the back wall.

"My buddy's mom had these in storage and they're too big for most houses these days. He thought they might work for displaying stuff."

Might work?

She was already envisioning jars of jam and scented candles, with colorful gourds on the sides, adding a touch of fall. "They're perfect. And I can paint them and distress them over the winter so they're vintage-looking for next year. Jax, I don't know what to say except thank you. Thank you so much."

* * *

Next year.

As her words registered, he fought off a wince. Was she seriously thinking about staying in business? With all the work that entailed?

As soon as that thought entered his head, he quashed it.

Who was he to advise her to sell? To get out of the apple business and live her life? He wasn't exactly the prime example of a take-charge person anymore.

But you could be.

And maybe you're closer to that goal than you realize. Why not call that guy in Seattle and check out that new therapy? You've got nothing to lose and everything to gain.

Libby spun in a circle, taking in all the changes. They'd kept it rustic, but added overhead lighting, the new shelving units, the cabinets and a check-out area with a long counter near the door. At the far end of the counter was another shelving unit, fixed to the wall. "This is a huge amount of display space, though. What do I fill it with?"

"Fall stuff."

"Yes!" She raised her hand and gave him a high five. "I can bring pumpkins and gourds and ornamental corn in. Straw bales and cornstalks."

"If you order the stuff, I'll get it over here."

"Does Glenn know about all of this? What you've done to his barn?" she asked.

He nodded. "He does. He's fine with it." He didn't add that his father had approached Glenn about the barn after they'd talked the day before. Glenn had not only agreed to the makeover, he'd sold them the barn on one condition: that Libby could use it until she was back in business up the road.

That had been an easy point of agreement if Libby didn't intend to keep growing apples. This way she fulfilled her grandfather's dreams while he was alive. But Jax read the temptation in her eyes as she looked around. "I can't believe this."

"Well, it gets you through this season with a solid look."

"Oh, it does way more than that," she told him and clasped his hand and when she did that, she clasped a piece of his heart, as well. "It gives me the possibility of re-establishing everything my grandparents loved and my parents hated. My mother thought a good reputation was a joke. It's not," she continued. "It's something special. Something to polish, and the O'Laughlins did that for generations until my mother came along. She seemed bent on making my grandparents' lives as tough as possible."

"And yours?"

The shadow in her eyes said yes, but she squared her shoulders and released his hand. "For a long time, yes. But I'm leaving that in the past, where it belongs, because I've got a whole life ahead of me. For me and CeeCee. If I dwell on the shadows of the past, how do I create a bright future for that wonderful little girl? With this I can put the luster back on the O'Laughlin name. That would be the perfect way to honor my grandparents for all they've done for me."

Her look of hopeful expectation didn't just touch him. It inspired him just enough to feel like an old wrench might be working on the tight clamp around his heart, which he hadn't let loose in three long years. "How soon can you have the pumpkins ordered?"

She pulled out her phone. "Now. But where can we get veggies for that pretty table out front?"

"Lincoln Washington's family said they'd supply us. They've got a major stand at the big farmer's market in Quincy, but they're always looking to wholesale some stuff according to Linc."

"You know the Washingtons?" She'd spotted a small pad and pencil on the countertop. She picked it up and began jotting notes as she posed the question.

"Yes."

"They're a great family."

They were, and this was a perfect chance to tell her who he was and how he knew the Washington family, and so many other families in the Quincy area. Because he was raised there, part of the sprawling Ingerson family, owners of CVF. How would she react? Would she want to protect Cleve from dealing with them? He couldn't fault her for wanting the old fellow's final days or months to be trouble-free, so in the end, he said nothing.

"I'll call Janas Farms up on Route 2. They grow everything you can imagine for fall decorations and for cooking. Do you want me to call the Washingtons?"

He certainly did not, and he'd have to warn Linc to keep their friendship on the down low. "I'll follow up with them. Are you ready to start sorting apples?"

It wasn't a big question, but the moment he asked her, her face lit up and he realized it was a very big question after all. "I've never been more ready in my life."

"Let's do this." For the next two hours

they bagged pecks and half pecks and packed green fiber quarts of Galas, Fujis and Granny Smiths. Once done, she moved on to sorting the thick-fleshed purple Italian plums, while Jax arranged the bagged apples along the new shelves.

The produce looked great. He stepped back to admire the display as she moved his way. Between the rows of freshly picked fruit and the scent of her hair, the smell of apples and autumn filled the well-stocked barn. She pointed to the customer-friendly top racks. "Let's leave a few random spaces for things like cake pans, pie pans, spices folks need for apple pies and pumpkin pies. I've got totes that Grandma had filled with great fall stuff. We'll put some nutmeg graters here, those small handheld ones, with jars of whole nutmeg right next to it. I can order that in bulk from the store in Wenatchee. We used to have this kind of thing when I was younger. Then I was gone, Grandma got sick and Gramps had enough on his plate to keep up with apples."

"An orchard that size is never a one-man operation. Especially at trimming and harvest times."

"He showed me how to trim this past winter."

That explained why the old-style dwarf trees looked as good as they did, as well as the abundance of nicely sized fruit on half the orchard.

"But I could see him failing once Grandma was gone. CeeCee was in preschool and he and I would go out into the orchard for hours, trimming, then clearing the paths. I knew he probably didn't have another season in him. So this..." She looked around the selling area. "This will delight him. I'm going to call in an order to Yakima, then pick it up this evening if they can have it ready." Her phone buzzed a reminder. "Oops, gotta get back. Mortie's due to leave. She's been training a health aide who'll be coming in for two hours a day, and CeeCee will be getting home soon. Jax." She touched his bare arm with her hand.

Her palm was cool after handling the chilled fruit. Despite that, his skin warmed and another part of that rusted lock on his heart busted loose. She met his gaze. "Thank you for caring. For doing all this. I don't know why God put you in our path that day. But you've made a tremendous difference to my grandfather, to CeeCee and to me. I can't tell you how much that means."

The sincerity in her eyes drew him. *She* drew him. But he knew better.

God hadn't put him in her path. That had been accidental timing. Nothing more. But he wasn't immune to the thrum of awareness that went straight from the touch of her hand to the beat of his heart. And while he understood the situation was impossible, she didn't. That meant he had to be the one to step back. He did, but it was the last thing in the world he wanted to do.

"Keys." He handed her a set of two keys as he shifted away. "They work on the front doors and the back door. I'll keep a key myself, if that's all right? That way if I have to get in here to move things around, I don't have to bother you."

She'd noticed the step back. She didn't react overtly, but when she gave him a simple nod, he knew and that made him feel worse. "Wise move. And then you can give it back at the close of the season. Or whenever we're done with the barn."

She walked out quietly.

It was better this way, but when she climbed into that old truck and drove away, he wanted things to be different.

They couldn't be because he wasn't the man she thought he was and a woman like Libby deserved the best. A man who could be trusted in all things. Right now, that wasn't him.

But that didn't stop him from wishing he was wrong.

Chapter Eight

There weren't many people at the town board meeting that evening. That should have calmed Libby's nerves, but when she spotted an ill-tempered neighbor in the front row, her anxiety increased. Lora Moore had purchased a four-acre plot with a small ranch house nearly two decades ago, and she'd been making trouble for people ever since. As a next-door neighbor, she left a lot to be desired. She'd had goats with bad fencing, two old sows that worked their way loose from time to time and a pony that had once caused a car crash. Fortunately, no one was badly hurt. Including the stubborn pony.

Despite being ticketed by the town multiple times, the middle-aged woman still had a menagerie—and an opinion on everything. Her presence meant she most likely had her own personal thoughts on their barn, and after a few dustups between Lora and Gramps over the years, Libby was pretty sure her neighbor might have an ax to grind.

The same could be said for her grandfather, but he wouldn't be here to speak for himself. It was up to Libby, and the thought of facing the old family foe made her gut clench.

The supervisor called the meeting to order. They went through the approval of minutes and the old business quickly.

Jax wasn't there.

She scanned the small room several times while the board conducted business, hoping he'd come soon.

When he didn't arrive, she gripped the

thin folder in her hands with tight fingers and a racing heart. When the supervisor got to her name on the agenda, she stood. Her knees wanted to shake.

She refused to let them.

Every person on this small-town board knew who she was. They knew her parents had scammed some local businesses by leaving town and never paying their bills. And her father had probably insulted most, if not all, of them at one time or another. One board member had even forbidden her children from playing with Libby back when they were children.

Stephie Rodas had been told to avoid Libby everywhere. In school. On the playground. At church, with Grandma and Gramps. And Stephie made sure everyone in the fourth grade knew it.

That's yesterday's news. Don't borrow trouble. Hold your head up high and stand your ground.

Grandma's words, and good ones. Libby lifted her chin, met the supervisor's gaze and indicated the folder in her hand. "I'm Libby Creighton from O'Laughlin Orchards, and I'm requesting approval to replace one of two barns that were destroyed in the windstorm we had."

The supervisor raised a copy of the plans. "We've got your plans, Ms. Creighton, and the board has a few questions for you. But first—" he leaned forward slightly "—we were all sorry to hear of the damage on your farm. We had a few damaged structures in town as well, and we're thankful no one was hurt."

"If people kept their places in better shape, these things wouldn't happen," snapped Lora from seven seats away.

"Ms. Moore, the public will have a chance to speak once Ms. Creighton has presented her request."

"Well, it's all right there in black and white, same as you posted in the weekly," she griped. Board meetings and agendas were publically posted for input, and it was clear that their eclectic neighbor had input. "I don't expect anything new has been added."

The supervisor aimed a firm look at Lora. "You know the rules, Lora. And we have your letter on the topic, as well. Let's move along."

She'd sent them a letter?

Of course she had, because she had nothing better to do than stir up trouble.

Libby worked to put a firm clamp on the rise of emotion.

The supervisor turned back to Libby. "You're looking at a pole barn, I see."

"Yes." Jax had offered to do this part. Fortunately she'd studied the plans to familiarize herself, so she launched into the details in what she hoped was a clear, calm voice.

Vanna Rodas seemed unimpressed. Lora Moore shuffled her feet with impatience at the other end of the front row.

She ignored them as she trained her attention on the other board members. They couldn't see that her palms were sweating or hear her heart beating a steel drum rhythm in her chest. And just as the board began asking some more technical questions, Jax walked in.

He took the seat to her right. But he didn't jump in to take over.

He sat there and let her answer questions.

And she did it.

He stepped in only twice: once to confirm load-bearing figures and once to address anticipated off-road parking during the season.

Then the supervisor opened the meeting for questions.

Lora stood right up. "Well, they tell you they've got the parking thing all worked out until you get to October and have people parking up and down the road, on both sides, mind you. It's a traffic hazard. I say they set the barn back another hundred feet, allow more off-road parking and save a possible accident. There is no way the rest of us can see properly to access the road during the entire apple season, and no town in their right mind can approve that. Not when you have a chance to change it."

A hundred feet back? That would mean taking out at least five Gala apple rows. That might seem like a small loss, but profit margins on a farm were tight. A bumper crop dropped prices while a poor crop drove prices up, so losing five rows of productive early-season trees was no small thing.

She started to respond but Jax put a hand on her arm. "May I?"

She didn't want to say yes. He'd deliberately backed off that afternoon and the sting of that rubbed raw. But he and his friends had done an amazing job on Moyer's barn so she put the lid on her ego and nodded.

He stood and faced the board. He'd said the board was accustomed to seeing him and their friendly greetings proved him right. He motioned to the plans in her hands, then to Lora Moore. "I think the neighbor's concern is justified."

Libby turned quickly, because it wasn't

justified. It was mean and spiteful because Cleve had chewed Lora out for letting her animals get into his carefully tended orchard and now she saw a way to get even. Everyone knew that folks frequented local farms and orchards during harvest time and drove accordingly.

"I've actually looked at the area for Cleve O'Laughlin and his granddaughter and we have enough room to move the barn back by sixty feet to the north and sixty feet west. That way we have more parking and better ingress and egress out of the orchard lanes. And a direct line to the back of the barn for apple storage."

He was right, there was room to do that now. And it wasn't as if they had to use the original barn's footprint or base. It wasn't the right size.

"That could allow Ms. Creighton to turn the concrete slab that had been the floor of the former barn into an outdoor selling area during the season, something that was impossible with the old barn's placement."

"I like that compromise." The supervisor turned toward the board. "Since we've already discussed and approved the plans, does anyone have further concerns to bring up before we vote?"

"I do." Vanna Rodas spoke quietly from the far end of the board's slightly elevated dais. "Ms. Creighton is not the owner of record. Her grandfather is and I'm sorry to hear he's in declining health."

When the bank officer had shared regret, Libby knew it was real. That wasn't the case now as she faced Stephie Rodas's mother.

"I'd like to know Ms. Creighton's plans for the future of the orchard."

She wanted to know Libby's plans? Why was that their business?

She looked from the supervisor to Vanna Rodas and back.

She started to stand, but the supervisor waved her back down. "That's got no point of reference for our approval or disapproval, Vanna."

"It has a bearing on our town, therefore it's justified," the woman argued. "If we approve this only to have a big fruit grower swoop in and buy the property at a handsome profit for Ms. Creighton, then we're offering a single citizen preferential treatment, aren't we?"

Libby couldn't stay silent any longer. She'd had to deal with Vanna's bias as a child. She refused to do it as an adult. "To replace a barn blown apart by a once-in-a-hundred-year windstorm?" She stood, ready to argue, but the supervisor made it a nonissue.

"That's not the board's call, Vanna. Our approval is based on town law. The presented plan meets all the requirements. I move that we put it to a vote."

"But—" Vanna's frown etched tight lines around her eyes and mouth.

"I second that motion," offered B.J. Johnson. He sent a smile of support Libby's way. And a wink. To her surprise, the wink and the smile soothed her.

"All in favor?" The supervisor was deliberately ignoring Vanna's protest, but why was she protesting in the first place?

Maybe it's not about you. Maybe she's just a jerk.

The barn was approved by a margin of six to one.

"Congratulations." Gert's husband stopped to shake her hand briefly as he headed for the door. "I've got to pick up Charlie and get him from football practice to his SAT prep class, but I'm glad this worked out, Libby. And Gert's been having a good time in that orchard. She says it's like old times, hauling sacks of apples."

"She's been amazing," Libby told him. "They all have."

"Well, she wants to be in shape for our daughter's holiday wedding, and she says this is accomplishing two goals. It's helping you bring in the apples and helping her stick to her new diet."

"Glad I could help." She smiled up at

him. "Your wife is a wonderful woman, Mr. Johnson."

"She sure is." He hurried off.

Lora had hustled out of the meeting once the vote was taken. She didn't say a word and Libby wasn't sure if that was good or bad.

But Vanna had stayed right there in her seat, staring at Libby.

Libby refused to look back, but she felt the older woman's gaze boring into her as she started to leave. A part of her wanted a face-off. The little girl she used to be wanted to know why Vanna was so mean.

But she wasn't a child any longer and Vanna had no power over her. She had her permits for a barn that might be sold in a year, but if having a barn nearby kept Gramps happy, then she'd have a barn nearby. Even if it took a large share of the harvest money. She'd scrimped and saved as long as she could remember. She could do it again.

Jax was waiting for her in the aisle. He

fell into step alongside her as she moved toward the exit. "Sorry I was late."

"It's fine."

He sent her a dubious look. "Your tone says it's not fine and you're right. I tried to get here and—"

She turned. "I said it's fine. I've been standing on my own two feet for a long while. I'd studied the plans, they were fairly basic and I handled the questions. It all worked out."

"Except you're angry." He moved forward to open the door for her.

She didn't want him to open the stupid door, and yes...she *was* angry.

Angry that small-minded people put deliberate roadblocks in the way of others. Angry that a grown woman didn't have the decency to treat her with respect. And yes—angry that he was late and hadn't bothered to let her know. "Long day and still stuff to do."

"Libby, I—"

She walked off because if she didn't, she

wasn't sure what she might say but she was pretty sure she'd regret it. By the time she got home, she'd cooled off enough to thank Mortie for coming over, tuck CeeCee into bed with one story and two prayers and a drink of water, and make sure Gramps was asleep. One positive of his illness was that he slept a good ten hours most nights, which was a much-needed breather at the end of the day.

She tucked the folder aside, walked onto the back porch and studied the orchard by the light of a full moon. The leaves glowed quicksilver in the pale glow. With the barn gone, she could just make out the late-variety trees in the distance, still heavy with fruit.

She was blessed by the harvest. Blessed by her sweet daughter. Blessed by so much.

And yet it was never quite enough, and Vanna's words brought that back tonight. She was instantly drawn back to the little girl whose parents didn't love her, didn't take care of her and shipped her to her grandparents because she was too much bother.

Had she been a bother to Gramps and Grandma, too? Did raising their granddaughter rob them of the chance to just be elders, unfettered by school schedules and a child's needs?

Why are you letting one sour person negate all the good people you've seen today? Mortie giving of her time and expertise. Gert and her bus-driving friends. Gert's husband and the town supervisor and all those board members who gave a quick thumbs-up to your project? And Jax with all of his hard work?

"Be still, and know that I am God."

The sweet, short verse said so much with so little. She needed to cling to that more often. To put aside the worries of the world and take heart in the stillness of God. Most times she was able to grasp that mentality, but she'd lost the grip when she faced Stephie's mother tonight.

No one can make you feel inferior without your permission.

She had the Eleanor Roosevelt quote on her bedroom wall, right above a picture of her and CeeCee in last year's ripe orchard.

She'd forgotten that resolve tonight. That was her fault.

Tomorrow she'd begin anew. She'd greet a brand-new sales season and apologize to the man who made it possible, Jax Mc-Claren. If her heart took a hit because he shied away from her, that was her problem. Not his. The last thing he deserved was for her to take cheap shots because her feelings got hurt. He'd been a true friend from the very first. Returning that favor was the least she could do.

Chapter Nine

The dream came that night. He'd hoped it was gone.

Nope.

This time it didn't roar up like a hungry lion. Tonight it crept up like a snake, insidiously, with flashback moments that could have changed lives if other decisions had been made. But they weren't and he viewed the faces in his dream until the most life-changing moment of all came along, when that helicopter began to fall out of the sky.

And he could do nothing to stop it. Again.

He struggled to wake up.

Sometimes he woke up quickly. Other

times the dream dragged him under, holding him captive while he struggled to grasp reality, and when he finally sat up, a cold, clammy sweat claimed him.

His heart raced.

His hands went numb.

He sat on the edge of the bed, aware of nothing but how absolutely alone he was. And how his choices affected others because he didn't take his place on that chopper.

He couldn't have stopped the crash. A mechanical malfunction caused the engine failure, and despite the experienced pilot's best efforts, the huge chopper wouldn't respond.

But Jax was supposed to be on it.

Aunt Connie believed God still had work for him to do.

His father agreed.

His therapist asked what he thought and Jax was pretty sure the words *pure chance* came out of his mouth.

Grandma Molly used to tell him Bible

stories all the time. She'd share the words with all three boys, and he bought into them from the time he was small until that mechanical bird fell out of a clear blue sky for no good reason.

He didn't care about those words now.

He knew what he wanted.

He wanted to be able to save his men and see them safely home six weeks later. It burned him that six short weeks had separated them from the rest of their lives and the life-stealing crash.

He couldn't change it.

But he couldn't seem to get over it, either, and maybe that was *his* life sentence. To face that day repeatedly, wishing he'd never sent those men off on that practice flight because if he hadn't, they'd all be alive right now. And he had no clue how to deal with the reality of that.

He didn't want to go to Libby's the next morning. He'd messed up the day before, and he didn't want to face that look of disappointment in her eyes again, but he'd given his word so he dressed for orchard work and climbed into his truck.

He pulled into the farm's driveway and parked as usual. The school bus hadn't come yet. CeeCee was dancing along the edge of the stone drive as if going to school was a celebration. Libby was smiling at the child's antics while they waited. It was a nice routine. Normal. And he hadn't felt normal in a long time.

"Mr. Jax!"

CeeCee raced his way as he stepped down from the truck. She was full of delight and he had to smile back, even though the last thing he wanted to do was smile. But he couldn't help it because her joy was infectious. "Hey, kid."

She twirled. "Do you love this dress so much?"

His smile grew on its own. "So much."

She beamed, matching her smile to his. "Because it's so special, right? And guess what. Guess why I'm wearing such a pretty dress today."

He didn't have a clue, but he tried his best. "Somebody's birthday?"

She laughed. "I love birthdays this much!" She spread her arms as wide as they could possibly go. "No, Mr. Jax, I get to wear it cuz it's not a gym day! When it's not a gym day I can wear a pretty dress because I don't have to run around and kick a soccer ball or climb ropes or do anything like that!" She planted her hands on her hips and spoke in the most adorable stern voice he'd ever heard. "I don't even like doing those things, I mostly like playing outside on the playground or climbing apple trees because they're just the right size, but my gym teacher makes us do ropes and stuff." She frowned and he was fairly amazed how quickly her features morphed from one emotion to the next. "But when he tells me to do it, I do it, because Mom says, 'CeeCee, you have to follow directions. When a grown-up tells you what to do, you do it.'"

"Moms are smart like that," he agreed as Libby drew closer.

Just then, they heard the rumble of the bus coming down the road.

He lifted CeeCee up and carried her to the road's edge, and when Gert pulled up he set her down and waved her onto the bus. And when all the kids on the bus began waving to him, he waved to them, too.

Their happy faces touched him. Their innocence soothed until the bus rolled away and Libby cleared her throat behind him.

He turned, ready to make his apologies.

She beat him to it. Meeting his gaze, she said, "I'm sorry I was a jerk last night."

Her words caught him by surprise. "You weren't."

She aimed a face of disbelief his way. "I totally was. I let one snippy person get under my skin and I should know better. I've worked hard to move away from things that trigger me and yet I still let it happen. I'm ashamed of myself because then I was short with you and you've been such a wonderful help to us. I'm so sorry and I'll try not to let it happen again."

"You have triggers, Libby?" He knew about triggers. He didn't like going into Seattle because the choppers along the water carried him half a planet away. If someone brought up questions about his time in the service, he walked away. He didn't talk about the war or his time in uniform. Ever. Oh, he knew about triggers, all right. But the thought of this kind, gentle woman having triggers made him want to fix them for her. And then keep her safe. "Why did it trigger you, Lib?"

She waved it off as if it wasn't a big deal, then he realized she was refusing to let it be a big deal. "Old stuff, best left buried. But maybe not buried deep enough if I let Vanna Rodas get to me like that. I kicked myself all the way home because I have so much to be grateful for and it's silly to let one person's bad attitude have that kind of effect on me. In any case—" she turned as if to go back to the house, then didn't "—

you've been nothing but good to us. To me, to CeeCee, to Gramps. And I let a little thing like being late to a meeting get under my skin. That's not like me."

That wasn't what got under her skin. Not the only thing anyway. Although neither one addressed it, he'd pulled away from a sweet moment yesterday and he'd seen the hurt in her eyes.

He knew it. She knew it. But a kind person like Libby deserved all the good things life had to offer. That didn't include night terrors and cold sweats. Or wanting to dive under cover when the beat of chopper blades filled the air. A woman deserved the best a man could be and he hadn't been that man for a long while, although sometimes—here on this farm, with Libby and CeeCee and the old fellow in need of a helping hand—he almost felt like he *could* be that guy again.

"You like your privacy."

She scrunched her face instantly. "A measure, yes. But it's mostly because I promised myself that I'd move on. Grab the future and leave the past behind. It's not worth thinking about or wasting time talking about because it is what it is. I can't change it, but I can make the future whatever I want it to be. So I don't ponder it." She flashed him a quick smile. "Not when there are apples waiting. Actually, the two fellows you hired should arrive any minute and I've got an order to pick up at Spragues and Janas's for the apple shop, so I'm going to grab Gramps and take him with me."

"And you're all right if I set up Quincy Construction to get going on the barn?"

"We have approval and some funding. And the apple sales will give us the rest, so yes. Let's do it."

He had no intention of using her apple harvest to pay for the barn, but she didn't need to know that yet. "I'll come get Cleve around noon or so. That way his lunch isn't delayed."

"Perfect. The home health aide gets here at noon and Gramps doesn't like to wait for meals," she agreed, and then she swung back his way.

So beautiful.

The light in her eyes was such a winsome joy that it was almost easy to forget that other look. The sad look he'd witnessed. What would it take to wipe that hollowed sadness away forever? He couldn't deny that he just might want a chance to do it.

He couldn't, of course.

His conscience scolded him quickly. *If you wouldn't set up roadblocks to your recovery, you might find a way. Set up an appointment in Seattle. You've got nothing to lose.*

He'd avoided some of the suggested therapies because no amount of talk or mumbo jumbo was ever going to erase the reality of what happened.

A puff of wind blew a strand of hair across Libby's face. He reached out and tucked that errant strand behind her ear. And then he left his hand there. Cradling one side of her head.

She stared up at him.

He looked back, the feel of her soft hair, the smooth cheek and her gentle beauty calling to him.

And then she stepped away. "We're not going to start something we can't finish."

Instantly he wanted to figure out a way to that finish line.

"Neither one of us is ready for something serious, and I don't do casual," she warned him. "Ever."

"That makes two of us, because I stay as far away from serious as I can get," he told her.

"Then it's good we understand each other." She said the words, but then she laid her hand over his. "Because I'm enjoying working with you. You've made a difference here, and I can't tell you how grateful I am. But I can show you," she went on.

He frowned.

"Have supper with us tomorrow night. We'll be busy at the new apple shop, then we can order pizza and celebrate our first weekend of the season."

"Only if you let it be my treat."

"Dutch," she proposed. "We split the cost."

"Uh-uh." She'd moved her hand, so he had to move his, but as he started for the apples, he took a parting shot. "I buy the pizza. You donate a jug of cider."

"Done." She smiled at him from her spot on the steps.

He smiled up from the driveway, and when she went inside, he grabbed a stack of sacks from the back porch and moved toward the orchard, whistling.

He'd been exhausted when he arrived. Worn. Drained.

He wasn't a bit tired now. CeeCee's excitement, Libby's grace, the beautiful day— had all energized him.

She said she'd moved on.

From what, he wondered? How bad could it have been?

He had no idea, but he knew one thing.

He didn't want anyone or anything to hurt her again. Ever.

And as long as he was around, nothing would.

No way was she ready for heartbreak.

Libby schooled herself as she backed the truck up to the apple barn's new front doors. Gramps almost jumped out of the passenger seat. His feet hit the ground and he hurried forward, excited. "Well, this is prettier than I remembered, isn't it? A sight prettier, and our name is on the barn." He spun toward Libby. "Who put our name on Glenn Moyer's barn?"

"Jax and his friends cleaned it up for us. They painted it and added the shelves and tables. Mr. Moyer said we could use his barn as long as we needed it."

"A good neighbor is a good friend by proximity."

"Wise words. I'm going to unload these things and stock shelves, Gramps. Do you want to look around?"

"I want to help," he declared in a voice that sounded like the old Cleve. Strong. Vital. Focused.

"I'd appreciate it," she told him. They unloaded bakeware and canning supplies to fill the new shelves. The cider delivery arrived while they were setting up. Libby showed them to the back door and they dollied the cases of fresh-pressed cider into the cooler.

She had them bring the last dolly into the front, and they had just left when Janas Farms arrived with pumpkins, gourds and cornstalks.

When Jax arrived at eleven forty-five, he swung into a parking spot, jumped out and whistled. "You guys moved all this stuff into place?" He motioned to the full tables and shelves. "Please tell me the delivery guys helped."

Libby flexed her right arm in a show of strength. "They got the stuff here," she replied. "The rest was me and Gramps.

But I'd love some help on that last pumpkin display."

"Not our first rodeo, son." Cleve grinned as he settled an armload of cornstalks into a stanchion. "We've done this kind of thing since Libby was real little. Nothing we haven't done before."

The lucid moment made her heart soar.

That was the real Gramps. A go-getter, a man who tackled whatever job came his way. The smile, the ease of motion.

This was how she wanted to remember him. And this was why Grandma made her promise to keep him on the farm if possible. There was no replacement for the joy in his face, in his gaze. As he helped Jax move the pumpkins into place, he moved with the agility of a younger man. For this moment, that was what he was. She snapped a few pictures with her phone, and a short video of their shared smiles and light repartee.

They finished arranging the pumpkins at twelve noon. "Cleve, I'm going to take you back to the house for lunch, all right?"

"I am hungry, that's for sure." Gramps turned quickly, looked at Jax, then frowned. "Who are you again? Did you come with that nice gal over there?"

And just like that, the moment was gone.

Jax sent her a look of sympathy.

He knew, she realized. Somehow he understood the roller-coaster ride she faced each day.

"I'm Jax, the fellow who's helping in the orchard this season. And I'll oversee the barn building, too."

"You're building a barn?" asked Gramps, perplexed.

Jax steered him toward the truck. "I'll explain while we head back to the house, okay?"

"I'm hoping there's tuna on the menu. Carolyn likes to make me tuna."

"Tuna sounds good," Libby told him.

"I'll bring back a sandwich." Jax shut Gramps's door and faced her before he moved to the driver's side. "It was a good morning, wasn't it?"

She nodded, fighting against the rise of emotion. "The best. And I'll take every one I get."

"Back soon." He climbed into the truck, drove down the road and was back in a half hour.

She'd finished the inside displays and was adding seasonal touches outside when he pulled in. He not only brought her a sandwich, he'd grabbed chips and fresh, hot coffee.

When he dropped the tailgate on his truck and pulled out a similar lunch for himself, she took a seat beside him.

The simplicity of eating a tuna sandwich and chips felt right. Sharing the moment with him felt right, too. She held up the second half of her sandwich and indicated her appreciation. "This is haute cuisine in my book."

"The same." He motioned toward the barn with his coffee. "I'm going to stay here for an hour, help you finish, then get back to the orchard. Courtney is with Cleve until two o'clock. The bus crew is picking the Granny Smiths, and they're quite excited about beating the two hired men, so the speed of today's picking is notable."

The image of the middle-aged bus drivers taking on the two young workmen made her laugh. "They challenged them?"

"Gert takes no prisoners," he replied. He was right, but Gert Johnson had another side, as well.

"That woman has the kindest heart in the whole valley," she told him. "She was my bus driver when I was little, she's been on the job for nearly thirty years and she always treated me with such thoughtfulness. When others brushed me off or didn't let me play with their kids, Gert was the soul of compassion. A kid doesn't forget people like that."

"Why wouldn't people let you play with their kids?"

He looked astounded, which meant he hadn't gone around asking about her or their family. She liked that. "My parents were notorious for drinking, doing drugs, swindling and outright stealing at times. My time with Grandma and Gramps was my respite, my safe haven. They loved me unconditionally. And when my parents were almost run out of town because of their misdeeds, Grandma begged them to leave me here. To let me stay at the farm."

"And they did."

She set the sandwich down for a moment. "They didn't. Gramps wouldn't give them money and they knew the best way to hurt my grandparents was to take me. Not because they wanted me," she said softly. "That had never been an issue. They took me away to punish Grandma and Gramps, then sent me back eighteen months later. So in the end, that chapter of my life turned out okay. After no small number of mistakes on my part. Now I'm where I should be, and I'm pretty sure it's exactly where I want to be. So maybe all is well that ends well."

Chapter Ten

Unwanted.

Uncherished.

Uncared for.

Jax had a hard time wrapping his head around that. What kind of heinous person treated a child like a commodity? He couldn't imagine it, but then he'd been raised by a loving father and a wonderful grandmother. "Libby, I'm sorry."

She shrugged and lifted the remainder of her sandwich. "It was wretched, but it made me stronger. Stronger within myself and stronger in my faith. Don't get me wrong," she went on, facing him frankly. "I hated parts of my life and I made some major mistakes. I was in a rough place emotionally a couple of times, but when I look back on that now, I realize I grew as a person. That doesn't mean I ever want CeeCee to face that kind of trauma. I've got the chance to give her a good, normal life and I intend to do it. But if iron becomes steel by being forged in the fire, so can I."

The candor of her words broadsided him.

His therapist had said similar things. He'd brushed them off as same old, same old and kept on doing exactly what he was doing now, moving from one quiet job to another, making no waves and absolutely no commitments.

But hearing her talk about being made stronger made him want to be stronger. Could he truly improve his mental state? Nothing had worked so far.

Maybe it didn't get better because your heart and soul had to heal first. Who puts a time frame on grief and pain? What if you just needed more time? Just because something didn't work the past few years, doesn't mean it couldn't work now. If you're willing to try.

It was eye-opening to him that Libby made him want to take a chance. He had nothing to lose by trying, right?

What if it fails again?

The dark thought encroached as he swigged the last of his coffee. He tamped it down.

Libby hopped off the tailgate, dusted off the seat of her pants and faced him. "Let's get a spot arranged for the Granny Smiths and we should pick at least enough Honeycrisps to make a display. I know they're a little shy of ready, but they'll ripen in the baskets. And thank you so much for the lunch, Jax. That was another wonderful surprise on a really good day."

He slid off the tailgate, too. "Courtney was responsible for the sandwiches, but I'll take credit for the chips and coffee."

She laughed.

That was when he knew it was worth the risk.

He wanted to inspire that laugh more often. To have a chance to look after her and CeeCee. And Cleve, too. She'd already faced losing her grandmother. She shouldn't have to deal with Cleve's illness on her own. "We'll get the Granny Smiths and I'll bring back a few crates of Honeycrisps. Then we'll be set for tomorrow's big opening."

She scrunched her face a little. "I'm not sure how big it will be because folks might not know we're here. If they heard about the barn they might think we can't open up. But word will trickle out and if we don't have a great opening weekend, I expect we'll be busy in October. It just takes a little time for news to travel and we're three weeks late already. Most fruit stands were up and running in late August."

"Better late than never."

"Exactly."

They worked side by side to finish things

up. She worked steady, like him. No rushing, no dawdling. The really nice pair of blue jeans topped with a red T-shirt added to the look of a perfect all-American apple season. She looked beautiful, focused and capable, and she clearly had an eye for merchandising because the new apple shop didn't just invite people in, it coaxed them to purchase with clever displays. So well-done. She'd said she loved the merchandising side of retail and it showed in the inviting details of each display.

His phone buzzed a reminder a short time later. "Gotta go. This looks amazing." He folded his arms and looked at the well-stocked sales space inside the barn and then at her.

"It *is* amazing." She spoke softly and he had to lean a little closer to hear her. "I don't even know what to say, Jax McClaren." She turned to face him and she was close. So close he could count the tiny points of ivory in her blue eyes. "None of this would have been possible without you."

He started to wave that off, but she ignored the gesture. "It's true," she insisted. "You quietly came on board like on one of those TV shows where people show up out of the blue and help someone out of a jam."

"I'm just a guy who happened along at the right time."

"Not *just* a guy." Still speaking softly, she reached out a hand to touch his arm. "A special guy. A guy who goes the distance. There's not a night that goes by when I don't thank God for sending you down that road at the perfect time, because having your help has made all the difference. And I wanted you to know that."

Her voice was melodic and soft yet strong.

Her touch like velvet against his skin, even though her hands put in a lot of work and effort day after day.

Suddenly, he just stopped thinking, leaned forward and caught her mouth with his.

She fitted. In more ways than he would have thought humanly possible. And when she didn't pull away, he slipped his arms around her. Jax was pretty sure he'd found everything he'd been looking for. When he paused, his heart was beating a mile a minute. So was hers.

He drew her into his chest and held her there, close and safe for long, beautiful seconds. "Well, then."

She started to pull back and he tipped his face down to catch her eye. "We can stop wondering now."

She raised a brow.

"About what it would be like if we kissed each other," he whispered. "Please don't tell me I was the only one wondering, because I don't know if I can take the shot to my ego."

Her blush confirmed what he already knew. He loosened his embrace but kept his hands looped lightly around her back. "And just so you know, it was better than I'd imagined, and I've been imagining a lot these last few weeks."

"Jax—"

Her voice held a note of caution. He leaned his forehead against hers. "I know there are a dozen reasons why we shouldn't do this, but I want to ignore every one of them and kiss you again, Libby."

"Like, once?" she asked, and he felt her lips curve in a smile.

He kissed her cheek. "Like, a lot more than once."

She laughed and drew back, but then she turned serious. "We're grown-ups, Jax. We both know the attraction isn't one-sided. But I've got a little girl up the road who thinks you're pretty special. I can tell you're her knight in shining armor right now, but she's the reason I don't date. Because she matters more than anything. She's already had to deal with a father who didn't care about her, Grandma's death and Gramps's condition." She eased out of his arms. "I won't deny the magnetism between us. But we can't be doing this again."

"And yet here I was wondering when we *could* do it again." He grinned down at her, not because he was all that funny, but because when he was around her, he wanted to smile. And often. Wasn't that a wonderful change?

The blush deepened. "Then stop thinking of it," she scolded lightly. "You've got to go."

He did have to leave. He'd promised the workers he'd be back. "We can discuss this later. Why don't we all go out for supper tonight? You, me, Cleve and CeeCee."

"We can't," she told him. "I'll be making display signs tonight. I want to hit the ground running tomorrow morning at the apple shop, even if it's not busy."

"I can help."

She'd turned away, but then she swung back. "Actually, you could. If you could entertain CeeCee and Gramps so I can have an hour with a permanent marker and card stock, I can get a whole lot more done than if I'm interrupted every five minutes."

"I'm happy to, Lib." She hadn't offered more about CeeCee's father, and he wasn't about to ask. A man with secrets had no right prying confidences out of another person. "See you later."

He climbed into the pickup truck, turned it around and looked back to wave goodbye.

She didn't look up. Didn't wave. Eyes down, she pretended to be busy, but as he turned the truck onto the two-lane, he glanced back at the same time she sneaked a peek in his direction.

He slowed down and smiled, then gave his roughed-up cap a light tap of the finger.

He couldn't see if she blushed again, but he saw the smile, and for now, that was enough. He drove up the road, whistling. He pulled into the driveway, ready to grab Cleve and join the apple crew in the orchard, except they weren't in the orchard. Ten people were scattering in multiple directions, all shouting Cleve's name, and when Courtney saw him, she raced his way. "He's disappeared, Mr. McClaren."

Jax's heart jumped into overdrive. They'd gone through this with Grandma Molly and he'd never forgotten those terrifying hours before she was found. "When did you first miss him?"

"Just now." Her voice shook. She fought tears, swallowed hard, then explained in a stronger voice, "I was tidying up the kitchen and bathroom areas. He was sound asleep in his reclining chair, and I don't know when he got up and went outside. I came back to check on him and he was gone."

Jax texted Libby instantly, Cleve's gone missing.

Her return text was short. On my way.

"The orchard's the most likely place," said Jax. "He knows it's harvest season and he wants to help. I know you were supposed to leave, but can you stay at the house in case he comes back or someone calls?"

Courtney nodded. "Yes."

"Libby will be here any minute. Tell her we're all out looking."

"I will."

He raced for the orchard. Thick leaves

and spreading branches made it impossible to see through the trees. He ran to the western end and began making his way down the fruit-laden rows, calling Cleve's name. It wasn't cold right now, but the upper thirties were predicted overnight. He paused and texted Libby again, I'm in the Pinks. I'll work my way back toward the house.

I'm here. Checking east of the house.

Would Cleve have wandered onto Glenn Moyer's land? Why would Cleve—Jax stopped himself right there. Better than most he understood the futility of applying rational thought to irrational people. Cleve might have gone in any direction, depending on his state of confusion. He followed the fruiting trees to the end, then came back in the next row. He couldn't assume that Cleve wasn't one row over just because he didn't answer his call, because a dementia patient didn't always react the way a normal person would.

He was on the third row when he heard another searcher's voice. That meant their comb of this end of the orchard was almost over. He got to the end of the trees. Thickening brush lay ahead as Little Fork Creek traveled toward the river below. In an arid land, the availability of water from the dams, creeks and rivers had allowed farmers and ranchers the chance to turn a dry valley into a fruit grower's paradise. He spotted one of the bus drivers emerging from the adjacent row. Sammy raised his hands and indicated his watch. "No one's found him, but we've got to get back to the bus garage. The buses pull out in fifteen minutes."

"We'll call for help, Sammy." Jax indicated the orchard with a thrust of his chin. This would be so much easier with four-wheelers or golf carts around, but the O'Laughlins had none of that here and it would take hours to get some from CVF. Hours they didn't have. He texted Libby, Drivers have to leave. Time for a Silver Alert?

She texted back quickly, Just called it in.

Let me know when the sheriff arrives.

Will do.

He stuck the phone away, walked back into the orchard, then paused, conflicted.

He scanned the area around him.

Nothing.

He called Cleve's name several times.

Still nothing, but as he started toward the orchard again, something held him back.

He walked toward the creek, yelling for Cleve. The beautiful day surrounded him. Fair sky spread in all four directions, the clear air laying groundwork for the projected cold overnight temperatures. Was Cleve strong enough to withstand a freezing night? More important, was the old fellow dressed warmly enough to be out in sixty-degree weather, let alone the midthirties?

He called for Cleve repeatedly as he

combed the thick growth along the creek. Right about now he could use a dog at his side. Flint had been an amazing tracker, a great dog, but even a family pet would be better at threading its way through the stand of creek brush than he was.

CeeCee would come home to fear and commotion. Libby's poignant words had hinted at past chaos in their lives and what little kid needed that?

He paused again, indecisive. He'd gone well up the creek and uncovered nothing. He stared hard through the brush, through the grasses, through the trees. The calm day gave the illusion of visibility, but army training had heightened the reality of search and rescue. It didn't take much for a person to fade into the obscurity of thick cover, and he was only one man hunting for a needle in a sixty-acre haystack, and that was only if Cleve didn't go off O'Laughlin land.

Libby's text pinged him. Sheriff is here.

Intuition told him to keep looking. Common sense said they'd need to join forces with the sheriff's department.

He started toward the house once more. The beautiful day mocked him. He'd been down this road with Grandma Molly. He knew the risks firsthand. They should have locked the doors, and if that didn't work, then they could have installed passkey locks. And why was cleaning up a kitchen more important than watching a fragile, elderly man?

His instincts suddenly stopped him in his tracks.

This was army training, tried-and-true. His brain alerting him to something he'd seen but missed.

He walked back toward the creek. He stared up and down, back and forth. No bit of color broke the haze of greens, golds, browns and tan. No thread of fabric clung to the brushy branches twining to and fro in some spots and leaving wide-open access areas in others. He studied the creek, wondering what had put his senses on high alert, and then he saw it.

Rustling leaves.

On a clear, calm day with scarcely a breath of wind, the leaves on the lower side of the thick creek bed were moving.

He pushed that way, calling Cleve's name. It wasn't easygoing at first, but when he finally broke through to the creek's edge, there he was, facedown, half his aged body submerged in the cold, running creek while one hand batted back and forth at a thin, low branch.

"Cleve!" He raced forward, drew the elderly man up and out of the water, then grabbed his cell to text Libby. I've got him. He was in the creek. Bring the truck and have an ambulance waiting. Facing north I'm at three o'clock from the last row of Granny Smiths.

I'm on it.

Short minutes later he heard the rumble of the truck engine. But he didn't wait. He'd stripped the old man's pants off and had wrapped him in his flannel, then bundled him over his shoulder in a rescue carry.

Libby and two deputies met him as he came through. "We've got him, Jax." Tug Moyer reached out. Tug's partner, Lorenzo, shifted more of Cleve's weight. "Let's get him out of here. Fire and rescue should be on scene momentarily."

Libby climbed into the truck bed and the two deputies helped Jax settle Cleve onto the hard surface. "If you go around the Galas, there are fewer bumps," Libby instructed him. "But you still have to go slow."

One of the sheriffs draped a warming blanket over Cleve, then they both climbed into the back of the truck, leaving Jax to drive.

He didn't want to think they might have been too late. Cleve's skin was cold. So very cold. And his eyes had wandered, then closed as if the incident had worn him out. He was edging the truck around the last row of trees as CeeCee's school bus pulled up and Rescue One turned into the drive. Sweet little CeeCee got off the bus to what had to be the worst scene imaginable. And when she jumped into his arms while the rescue workers worked on her ailing grandfather, Jax wanted to be able to offer words of reassurance and comfort, but Jax had absolutely no idea what to say, because if he'd gotten back to the farm ten minutes sooner—

The ten minutes he'd spent kissing Libby Creighton…

He might have spared them all.

Chapter Eleven

She'd been kissing Jax while Gramps had stumbled into the creek and nearly died.

What was the matter with her?

Libby put her head into her hands as she sat in the small ER waiting room.

She knew better. Sure, it would be easy to put the blame on Jax for being absolutely marvelous and wonderful and appealing. And kind and compassionate.

Don't forget incredibly handsome.

It didn't matter. None of it mattered. She'd broken the promise she made to Grandma, the one that said she'd take care of Gramps. Epic fail.

And she'd broken the promise she'd made to herself, to stay away from romance and all its potentially disastrous results so she could put CeeCee first.

"Please tell me you are not sitting here blaming yourself for this, Libby Creighton." Mortie's voice drew Libby's head up as the kindhearted nurse settled into the seat next to her. "I do believe we just had a talk about Cleve's impish tendencies, and how this was the most dangerous phase yet. Which means I should have had you put different locks on the doors to make it harder for him to slip out, and I should have done that when that windstorm blew through. I am so sorry, Libby." She drew her brow down, contrite. "Jax called me and said he'd go ahead and get it done if it was all right with you."

He'd texted her, asking permission. She'd ignored the texts on purpose because she'd already let him too far into their lives. And yet, this was something that needed to be done. Was she going to let foolish pride and guilt get in the way? No.

She nodded. "Yes, it's fine. Actually..." She took a deep breath, swiped her eyes and blew her nose on the clutch of tissues in her hand. "It would be a great help."

Mortie texted Jax, then put the phone away. People lined the walls of the waiting room, and the back-to-back double row of chairs along the middle was full. Almost everyone had a phone in their hand.

Not Mortie. She touched Libby's arm, closed her eyes and prayed in a low, crooning voice.

A couple of people glanced their way, then went back to their own lives.

"Lord, You delivered us into good hands, stable hands, educated hands. We ask that You bless those hands working on our beloved Cleve. Help him to know our love and feel our devotion through these works of mercy. We ask this in the name of our sweet Lord, Jesus."

Gert Johnson came in then. She crossed

the room quick and firm, the way she always moved, crouched down and bundled Libby into a big hug. "I am so sorry, sweet girl. So sorry. I wish one of us had seen him trekkin' that way, but it's deceivin' how thick and broad that apple foliage can be. How's he doin'?" Sympathy warmed her honey-brown eyes as she clutched Libby's hands in hers.

"Holding his own," Libby replied. "They're warming him with heated blankets and a saline solution. He's sound asleep and he looks so tired." Tears filled her eyes as she fought what she didn't want to say. "Maybe too tired."

"Oh, child." Mortie slung her arm around Libby. "There's no rhyme or reason with this disease and it's a hard road to choose when we ask for the Lord's help. What exactly do we pray for? Living brings a long and painful walk, but when we're not ready to say goodbye, the suddenness of loss hits us hard. I can't say I know which is better, so I leave it to God and I help and pray."

"Like you always have. Both of you," said Libby. "From the time I was little, you two have stood beside me and encouraged me. And I'm blessed to have you here now." She reached out for a group hug, then stopped.

Her heart stopped, too, as if it just couldn't go on beating anymore, until it rebounded in a clench of anger. There, a dozen feet away, was her mother. Standing there. Watching them. And she had the audacity to look sad, as if any of this mattered to her. What a joke.

Gert spotted Dianna, then stood up.

Mortie did, too, but she didn't look nearly as surprised. She reached a hand toward Libby.

Libby ignored it. Head high, she walked straight across the small but full waiting room and confronted the woman who dumped her all those years ago. "Get out of here."

Dianna Creighton flinched. Then she looked to Mortie for help.

Libby turned back to Mortie. "You called her?"

"I had to. Your grandfather's wishes. He wrote it in the instructions he has with his DNR. He didn't want anyone to go to extraneous means to keep him alive but he said he wanted one last chance to see his daughter before he went home to Jesus."

His daughter.

Libby's heart clenched. So did her gut.

After all these years, and all the bitter disappointments, Cleve still longed for that final moment with the woman who shamed her parents, hurt neighbors and friends, and used Libby as a pawn to try to get money out of Grandma and Gramps.

Her stomach heaved.

Prickles of cold raced up her back despite the warm room.

There were three people she never wanted to see again: her abusive ex-husband and her parents.

Her throat went tight. Her hands grew clammy. "I've got to get out of here."

"Come on, baby." Gert took her arm. "Let's you and me take a nice walk around the hospital. Mortie's got this."

"I'll text you any changes."

She couldn't answer Mortie. Not with knowing she'd brought Dianna there intentionally. And would Gramps even know her if he woke up?

Maybe. Maybe not. And when had she moved close enough to get here within a couple of hours? She'd been content to imagine her mother still in Southern California, although there'd been no contact in years. She could have been living nearby all along and Libby wouldn't have known it.

"Funerals and weddings, darlin'." Gertie clung tight to her arm as they made their way down a hall leading to the main lobby. "It's like the Lord Himself gives us opportunities to make peace at the times when folks gather. Of course, I've been to a couple of both where that particular notion didn't go well, but if your grandpa wanted a chance to make peace or offer forgiveness, he should get it because who wants to go home to the Lord with that weight on the soul? Not when sweet Jesus Himself told us to forgive seventy times seven."

"Gertie, I hear you." Libby knew the drill, and she believed, but when faced with a wealth of past emotions, it was a whole other story. "I know the rightness of it from God's vantage point, but the minute I saw her I wanted to have a knock-down, drag-out fight. I didn't want to forgive. I just wanted her out of my life like she did to me when I was twelve years old. So how do I shove all that aside? And how did she get here so quickly?" she wondered aloud. "That means she lives close enough to have made peace whenever she wanted. But she didn't."

"Maybe she couldn't." Gertie spoke softly as they passed a group of medical professionals. "It takes courage to go face-to-face with our indiscretions. So maybe she moved close enough to be on hand if needed, or to keep an eye on things and not intrude."

"The mother I know wouldn't do that." Discretion and compassion had never been part of Dianna's makeup. "Except I don't really know her at all because she tossed me aside once my usefulness ran out. You're giving her way more credit than she has ever deserved."

"Then we pray, Libby." Gert squeezed her arm lightly. "Not just for her, but for us, for us to deal with all those old feelin's. I know what you came from." Gert paused and faced her fully. "I know what I saw when I picked up a little girl from the Elm Street apartments. Unwashed. Uncared for. Unfed, likely as not, which is why I made sure my little basket had those crunchy bars you liked so well, and the fruit snack packs. And when I did see your parents, they were either hungover or gettin' ready to be hungover. I understood full well because my mama was the same way. Too busy livin' on the edge to take care of two kids." She looped her arm through Libby's again. "You and me, we moved on. Folks called me self-made but I told them it wasn't up to me. It was me and God, 24/7."

"You paid it forward by your kindness to me. And probably others."

"When I was hungry, you gave me to eat." Gert paraphrased the Lord's words in a warm voice. "So here's what you need to do. You don't owe anybody a thing. You don't owe that woman back there the time of day if it will bring you down because you need to be on your game for Cleve, for that farm and especially for CeeCee."

Gert's words surprised her. And then she went on to explain.

"But you *do* have to respect your grandfather's wishes. He's stood by you with lovin' care for a long time and I know they would have stepped into that bad situation you had in Seattle if they'd known. For a man to harm his wife goes against everything we've ever been taught, and your grandma cried many a tear over that when you got here. She had no idea that was going on."

"I was good at fooling people. Until the

end," Libby said softly. She didn't revisit that last year of a horrible situation often, mostly because she couldn't believe she let it go on for so long. The shame of that bit deep. "And then there was no possibility of fooling anyone."

"Why we feel the need to hide our wounds and mistakes is a problem," Gert said firmly. "Abusers are good at what they do. They're good at separatin' their victims from family and friends who will disapprove or ask questions. Carolyn realized that once you were back here, but when you didn't come back for visits or holidays, she thought you'd just turned your back on them."

"Like my mother. Only I'm nothing like her."

"And that's what caused her deep regret," Gert explained. "Because she knew that, but she took a burn when you wouldn't bring CeeCee to visit, like it was an insult to her and Cleve. She died still asking

God's forgiveness for not gettin' herself involved sooner."

Poor Grandma. Taking the weight of Libby's bad choices on her shoulders when she'd warned Libby to think twice about her choice of husbands. Her warnings had just made Libby dig her heels in further.

She understood things better now. A year of therapy painted a clearer picture. The younger Libby had been so desperate for love that it was easy to ignore the warning signs.

Young and foolish. But not anymore. "I don't think I can forgive her, Gert." It was a rough admission because her faith embraced mercy and unity.

"Well, that's between you and your mom and God, but that's not our focus right now, is it?"

It wasn't. Her focus was giving Gramps the best final days or weeks or months as God allowed. "No. So I'll play nice for Gramps's sake. It's funny that she didn't show up when Grandma died, isn't it?"

Gert clucked her tongue to the top of her mouth. "Well, your grandma was not one to be easily snowed and her tongue got tart towards the end."

"And I expect she didn't leave any such note for Mortie, because if she had, Mortie would have followed through."

"As she should."

Her heart had calmed down.

Her throat wasn't tight anymore and she didn't feel like retching.

She'd handle this for Gramps's sake because she loved him and respected his wishes. "I wish he'd warned me."

"Well, I can tell you why he didn't, most likely," Gert declared. "Why have you worryin' about a confrontation in advance? And why make you fret because who was to say Dianna would show up? No, he kept it to himself so that you could be at peace, Libby. Because he loves you that much."

He did. He always had. And as they made their way back to the waiting room, she made a firm resolution to God.

She might not be able to forgive her mother's selfish acts, but Gramps deserved every possible chance to reconcile with his prodigal daughter. And she'd be a wretched person to stand in the way of that.

She drew a deep breath, then pushed through the double doors leading into the waiting area.

She walked in, head high. She'd do what she had to do for now because it was right. Then she'd quietly close the door on that chapter of her life. Her mother had never once requested forgiveness, not like that was a big surprise. And if she did?

Libby was quite afraid that she'd never actually be able to do it. And that put the onus squarely back on her shoulders.

Chapter Twelve

The local news labeled Jax a hero for finding Cleve and bringing him to safety.

A small group of local news media had shown up as Rescue One pulled away, and the reporter had done a clever job of winnowing information out of the people there. They'd interviewed the responding sheriff, added in a doctor's warning about safety precautions to employ when caring for Alzheimer's patients and the cameraman had gotten several shots of him holding CeeCee in his arms.

He hadn't needed to say a word because he was no hero. If he hadn't delayed his return to the house by kissing Libby, he'd have been there and the old fellow wouldn't be fighting for his life right now.

CeeCee was tucked into bed, sound asleep. The bungalow-style house was quiet around him, and the chill of the autumn air quieted the night, a sure sign that change was in the air.

He'd cleaned up the kitchen and straightened Cleve's sitting area. Cleve liked his magazines just so, and his reading glasses to the left of them, although he didn't seem to do much actual reading these days. Still, he liked his personal order of things, and Jax understood the importance of that.

He'd just folded Cleve's favorite afghan when a knock sounded at the side door. He crossed the two rooms and checked the driveway from the kitchen window.

His father stood at the door, waiting.

Jax crossed to the door and yanked it open. "Dad."

"Getting cold out here." Richard Ingerson stepped into the side entry. "Got any coffee?"

"I can make some, sure. I don't generally drink it this late."

"Me, either, but tonight promises to be one of those times I make exceptions." His father clapped him on the back. "Any word on Mr. O'Laughlin?"

"Holding his own, they're raising his temperature gradually." He knew that because Mortie had texted him. Not Libby. "How did you know?"

His father hooked a thumb toward the small television across from Cleve's chair. "Caught half the news alert on Channel Nine. Saw you. And when you weren't at the cabin, I figured you must be over here or at the hospital."

Jax indicated a magnetized picture of CeeCee on the fridge. "Her mom's with Cleve. There's no family around to watch her and it didn't seem right making a five-year-old sit around a hospital for hours."

"So you stepped in."

"Wasn't much choice," he told his father

as the coffee brewed. "And even if there was, I'd have done it."

"You've been that way since you were born, Jax." Richard took a seat at the worn kitchen table and seemed quite comfortable there. "You're a protector. A nurturer. Great qualities to have."

"Well, I messed up today." The rich scent of fresh coffee tempted him. He didn't drink caffeinated beverages after two in the afternoon because he had enough trouble sleeping at night. Why risk more? Sure, maybe the circumstances offered an allowance tonight, but he'd been scripting his life and habits with care for three years. The firm schedule kept him grounded and focused.

"You saved a man's life today," said Richard softly. "Don't minimize it, son."

"If I'd gotten back to the house when I was supposed to, this might not have happened, Dad. I got here ten minutes late and Cleve had disappeared."

"Making this your fault won't help you or anyone else, Jackson."

He knew that, but—he couldn't stop feeling like it was.

His father went on. "Sometimes things just happen. If we govern ourselves by the what-ifs, we spend our whole lives questioning. Nothing is foolproof. The news report said there was a home health person on hand, watching over him."

"Doing dishes." His frown deepened. "Why would dishes be more important than looking after a real, live person?"

"You don't multitask?"

Jax growled because he always multitasked. He'd done it all his life; it was his way. He'd never minded having multiple plates spinning in the air, and he rarely let one fall. "Dad—"

"My mother was like an escape artist before her disease progressed to keeping her in bed." Richard sipped his coffee and sighed. "She slipped out time and again. It was like having a preschooler running around but she was tall enough to reach locks and maneuver them. That's why your aunt Connie gave up her job to stay with your grandma Molly. We paid her as if she was a regular employee because she had two girls to raise, but we couldn't leave Grandma Molly unwatched. And still she managed to give Connie the slip now and again. The sad truth is that most people don't have the financial option to make choices like that. Fortunately, we did."

He'd been in college for some of that time, but his father's words struck a chord. "Remember that time when I tracked her down at the rail station?"

Richard hiked both brows. "That was a scare. Fortunately she remembered how to drive for those few hours and got there safely. She used to oversee fruit shipments for the company back in the fifties and sixties, and she'd told you about that and you put two and two together."

Jax brushed the praise aside. "It wasn't

rocket science, Dad. Anyone could have done the same."

His father's forehead creased. "Not true. No one else took the time to listen to her ramblings. To help her out into the gardens she loved, or to take her for walks in the orchards."

"She liked the plums best."

"They were her favorite." His father's face eased into a smile. "And our new variety is named Molly May after her. She had an eye for fruit and a heart for God."

Faith-filled.

Jax hadn't thought of it in a while. Thinking of it now, the serenity of her face warmed his memories. "She liked going to church."

"With or without family, that woman stood solid for three generations of Ingersons and McClarens."

"And she never got mad at God for letting her get sick. Even when she was cognizant enough to know what was happening."

"Well, it wasn't God's fault, so why lay

blame?" asked his dad. "Do we throw blame at God for human frailty? Or because our bodies don't last forever? We're not perfect."

He started to answer, but his phone buzzed a text from Libby. He grabbed up the phone and read the message quickly. Waking up somewhat. Befuddled, but temp rising. Prognosis is better.

He texted back quickly, Good news! CeeCee is asleep. All quiet here. He hit Send and set the phone on the table.

He wanted her to text back. He wanted her to forgive him for being late…

Not for kissing her, because that had been absolutely wonderful, as if he'd come home to a place he'd never been. A place that beckoned with the peace and hope he'd lost years before.

The phone sat silent, and his dad had just poured a second mug of coffee when a soft *ping* indicated a new text. He tried to be casual, but when he snatched the phone off the table, he couldn't miss the slight smile that softened his father's face which meant he still couldn't fool his dad. He read the text, and as he did, his shoulders relaxed. So did his mind.

Thank you for staying. For finding Gramps. For being you. I would have lost him today if it wasn't for you, and I'm not ready for that yet. I want some more time to say goodbye. To give him one last earthly harvest. Bless you, Jax McClaren.

She wasn't blaming him.

She was blessing him.

The gentleness of her heart humbled him. He wasn't sure what to text back. He wanted to apologize, he wanted her forgiveness, he wanted—

I heard the news station called you a hero, she texted again. And this grateful apple farmer can't disagree. I'll talk to you in the morning.

No anger. No accusations. No finger-pointing, so why was he doing it to himself?

He hauled in a breath, then texted back, We've got tomorrow covered. You hang tight with Cleve.

She replied with a thumbs-up emoji.

His father stood. "I'm going to get on my way so you can get some sleep. You're going to need it for tomorrow. I may have quietly placed a few ads around town to let people know about the O'Laughlin apple stand reopening."

"Is that code for an advertising blitz?" asked Jax with a smile.

His father didn't say no, which generally meant yes. "Just wanted to get the word out, with them starting so late in the season. And because it was the right thing to do. You might need some help on hand. Should I send over a couple of workers from Quincy?"

If Libby came by and found Ingerson employees at the barn, he'd be outed instantly. "I think the crew from the bus garage can handle it. We'll pause picking for the weekend."

"Good strategy." Richard grabbed him in a hug. "You did well today, son. I'd give anything if you could see that the way I do."

He almost did. Hearing it from others, from his dad and then Libby, he realized that if three people are telling you the same thing, and you still disagree, then maybe your personal perception has gone awry. "My therapist would agree."

"She's a smart lady."

So why had he spent the last year ignoring her advice? First thing tomorrow he was making that call to Seattle. If the new PTSD video therapy helped, then good. And if it didn't, he'd lost nothing but some time. It was time to take the advice seriously. Time to act.

Richard tugged on his hat. "I'll talk to you tomorrow night, see how the opening day goes."

"Thanks, Dad." He hugged his father again. Just because. "I'm grateful for everything."

"That's what family's for, Jax." His father

walked outside and pulled the door snugly shut behind him. He climbed into his white truck with the familiar CVF logo on the side and pulled out, then headed home.

Jax crossed the living room, went upstairs and checked on CeeCee. She'd kicked off her covers. Tearstains tracked her cheeks from tears she hadn't let him see or hear. He drew the covers up lightly and touched her head. So sweet. So innocent. So full of life. But he was pretty sure she'd had a tough road the first few years on the planet.

What would it be like to make sure the rest of her life was good and solid? What would it be like to let himself care again? To put others first? To come out of hiding?

He tucked her fluffy black-and-white stuffed dog next to her, and went back downstairs. He grabbed a couch pillow and a bright-toned afghan, then sacked out on the couch. He wouldn't sleep.

He didn't dare. What if he woke up screaming with CeeCee upstairs? But he could rest his eyes, so that's what he did.

When the alarm on his phone chimed six hours later, he woke up, surprised and pleased. But one look at the time had him brewing coffee quickly. Libby had planned to make signs for the apple store. That hadn't happened.

He hunted up a permanent marker and a stack of card stock from a pile near the printer. One by one he wrote out signs and prices. By the time CeeCee got up, he had the signs done, and it was time to head up the road. She came downstairs quietly. He headed her way and lifted her up. "Hey, pretty girl. That's quite the outfit you've got on." She'd picked an interesting combination of stripes and florals with an apple-red vest over it. A miniature pair of Western boots completed the outfit. For all the crazy patterning, she looked absolutely wonderful.

"Is my mommy here?" she asked, looking over his shoulder toward the kitchen. There was no missing the concern in her tone. "And my grandpa?"

He was about to tell her no when a text came in. He saw the image and held it up for her to see as he read the accompanying text. Coming home midday. Gramps is so much better! He misses you, CeeCee!

"Oh, I miss them, too!" She dropped her head against his chest like she'd done the day before, and the rusty latch on his heart creaked open even more. "Tell them I miss them but I'm going to help you get the farm stuff done. Okay? Then they won't have to worry the littlest bit. Not if you and me work on stuff together!"

"I'll tell her," he promised. "What do you want for breakfast and can you eat it on the way? Because we need to head over to the barn."

"Apples!" She fist pumped the air. "My mom says the one good thing about apple farmers is they can't ever go hungry as long as they've got apples and a cooler."

"Then we've got a barn full of meals waiting for you." He texted Libby back quickly, Heading up the road now with

CeeCee. We're double-teaming the apple barn today.

Thank you!

There was no time to say more. He grabbed a box of granola bars as backup, tucked CeeCee into his truck with her booster seat and drove up the road.

Gert's husband pulled in right behind him. "Gert's still at the hospital with Mortie and Libby, so I said I'd work the stand."

"Thank you," said Jax, and he clasped the older man's hand in a quick gesture of respect as two more bus drivers rolled in. They parked around back, and by eight thirty, they'd put signs on everything, moved small wagons out front for customers' use and by eight forty-five the parking lot was full.

He swung the doors open, and as the day raced forward, he and CeeCee helped customer after customer with the bus drivers' help, as two of the men kept replenishing stock from the back cooler. In all his days, Jax McClaren had never seen so many happy faces. And all because they were shopping for apples at a simple road-side stand.

Chapter Thirteen

Libby couldn't believe her eyes when she approached the apple barn midafternoon. Cleve was tucked at home. Mortie had offered to stay with him while Libby helped at the apple stand. The bighearted nurse had practically shooed Libby out of the house once Gramps was settled.

Cars, SUVs and pickups filled the parking area and lined the street. She took the farm access trail bordering Moyer's land and drove around back, thinking she'd park behind the barn, but that was full, too. Finally she parked along the grassy area fronting the bare, fumigated land and was surprised when three more vehicles followed her right in to snatch a spot alongside her old truck.

She climbed out, waved a greeting to the new customers and headed for the barn.

Organized chaos welcomed her.

Dave and Jim, two of the helpful bus drivers, were busy restocking apple displays that sold as quickly as the men filled them. Half of her syrup and jam display was wiped out, and when she looked for the backup stock she'd stacked behind the new wall, it was gone.

All gone.

She turned in disbelief, and the first thing she saw was Jax's big smile. CeeCee was snug in his left arm and she was telling someone a story—

No shock there...

And the customer was listening.

Then CeeCee spotted her. "My mommy's here! Mommy, come look at all the stuff we're selling, and people are so happy to come see us and buy our apples!"

Folks heard CeeCee's invitation and turned. Instant heat infused Libby's face.

She'd never liked being the center of attention. CeeCee gravitated to it, but the thought of all these people watching her—

She was sure her heart was about to implode, but then a woman nearby touched her arm. She turned.

An old classmate stood there. Cass Summers, a quiet girl who sat on the far right in sixth-grade English and Social Studies during those dreadful years with her parents.

"Libby, I'm Cass Summers. Well, Cass Bradley, now." She indicated two busy boys playing checkers on a wooden table using miniature pumpkins.

"I remember," said Libby. But the question was, what did Cass remember? A kid coming to class in unwashed clothes when she was with her parents? Or the cleaner, nicer version when Libby lived with her grandparents? Seeing her mother had dragged up every possible bad memory she had, it seemed.

"I love what you've done here," Cass continued. "My kids are over the moon. We've grabbed pumpkins and cornstalks and apples, cider and cheese. This is amazing! It's gotten so hard to find an affordable place to bring the kids to give them a farm experience." She reached out and gave Libby a spontaneous hug. "I was sad when I saw what happened to your barn, but this…" She motioned to the sales area. "This is the kind of place we'll come back to. Thank you for creating the kind of place I can bring my kids to again and again. I know it couldn't have been easy."

She moved away as CeeCee threaded her way through the people. "Mommy!" She did her customary leap into Libby's arms. "Did you bring Grandpa home? Is he feeling better? Is he so happy to be home?" She lowered her voice into a fake monster tone as she asked, then smooshed her mother's face between her two small hands as if that would help Libby answer.

She moved CeeCee's hands away and

kissed her cheek before answering. "He's home, he's feeling better and he's promised not to go wandering again." She added that last as Jax drew near. "A promise he will forget, I'm sure."

"Not to worry. We installed new locks on the doors last night," he told her. "After things calmed down. And they're coded so he can't just open the door. I put them low enough so CeeCee could enter the code. We just can't tell Gramps what it is," he added.

"I promise!" CeeCee grinned up at him.

"Are there more Galas?" asked a woman nearby. "I like the lunchbox size—they're perfect for kids."

"We'll bring them right out." Dave had just emptied a dolly of apples. He tipped his cap to her and hustled into the back of the barn.

"You take over out here." Jax started to slip by her. "I'll help keep things stocked."

"Jax."

He'd almost gotten by, but he turned back the moment she said his name. She motioned to the crowd of people. Happy, laughing, talking people. "I don't know how to thank you."

"I do." A wide grin brightened his eyes. "Take care of these people so I can take a break. I haven't talked to or been pleasant to this many people in one day in, well…" He pretended to think. "Ever. Tag. You're it."

She laughed.

It felt good to laugh and talk with people and take care of their orders. CeeCee had clearly jumped right into her role of being the resident charmer, and as she jabbered off apple specs to customers, Libby was amazed at what the kindergartener remembered.

By six o'clock the store looked beat.

Apple stock of the early varieties had been hit hard, but the abundant harvest meant there were dozens of crates tucked in the conditioning cooler. Plums had been wiped out, all but the late varieties, and their festive autumn displays would need to be rebuilt because happy customers had picked them clean.

As she began a list, a Janas Farms truck pulled in to drop off more fall produce.

She turned toward Jax as he helped Dave unload the last of the prebagged apples onto display tables. "You called Mark Janas?"

"I hope that's all right," he replied. "I could see what was happening, so I gave them a shout midday. And even though we don't open until eleven tomorrow morning—"

Sunday mornings had always been a church-first schedule, even during the busy apple season.

"I wanted to get a jump on the day and restock as much as we could tonight. Did I overstep my boundaries?"

"Overstep?" She breathed out a sigh as she kept filling displays. "Not at all. I'm glad you thought of it. But you've got to be exhausted. Gert texted me that she's with Gramps right now. She sent Mortie home. And you've been at this all day. CeeCee,

too. I think you should both take a rest because we might be breaking Washington
State child labor laws."

Jax didn't seem worried about CeeCee's
involvement. "She loves this. She's totally
in her element. Still, she probably does need
to eat something other than apples and granola bars, so we'll head back to your house
for food once the pumpkins and vegetables
have been unloaded. Will Cleve be all right
with a bunch of us there?"

"As long as we keep it brief," she decided.
"Gramps loves a crowd. That's where
CeeCee gets it from." CeeCee was now ex-
plaining her goal of getting a dog to anyone who would listen. "I'm better behind
the scenes. So was Grandma. But Gramps
loved interacting with the public."

"I think you were amazing out here." Jax
stopped talking long enough to move the
dolly of apple crates up the row. "Totally
on your game. Extrovert at work."

When she made a face, he raised an eye-
brow. "I'm the opposite of that actually,

but none of that mattered when I walked in here and saw Gramps's dream coming true. A place alive with happy people, excited over pumpkins and apples. It was like when I was little, before he had to go head-to-head with big producers and corporate greed. He'll love seeing this. This is how Gramps sees farming and orcharding. You've set this up to make him very happy, Jax, and I can't begin to thank you enough. You've made an amazing difference here, and we're all grateful."

The others had gone outside to help unload the produce truck that had backed up to the pumpkin display. He stopped packing apples onto tables and turned her way. "Except that if I'd gone right over to your house yesterday, Cleve might not have gotten outside. If I hadn't stopped to kiss you, I might have spared an old man a lot of grief."

She faced him squarely. "I thought the same thing at first, but then I realized that Gramps is going to be a full-time job no matter what. As tough as that is, all we can do is our best. I'll bring him here with me every day. Just being around his apples and people might make a difference, but I'm also looking at the reality of the situation." She hadn't wanted to get into this now, but there really wasn't a way out. Yesterday's scare had shown her that. "Gramps has a DNR."

Jax's nod indicated he understood the implication of that.

"He doesn't want extraneous means. He made it clear in his papers that if God calls him home…" The words made her throat go tight, but she fought the rise of emotion. "He's ready to go. But if we can give him a beautiful season to remember, that's the best send-off there is. Gramps has always been a worker bee," she went on. "It would stress him more to see work left undone and fruit being wasted than it would to see a vibrant business flourishing around him. And as for that kiss?" She tucked one last full-peck bag onto the Granny Smith display and decided to go for the truth. "I thought it was downright amazing and I was kind of hoping you felt the same."

His quick frown made her heart plummet. Maybe it wasn't the same for him. Maybe—

He reached out and lightly grazed her cheek with his hand. "On a ranking scale of one to ten, I put it at a firm fourteen, Libby." His frown turned into a quick, teasing smile. "Just so you know."

The afternoon work crew was headed their way. She dipped her chin as her cheeks warmed. Time for a change of subject. "For now, I'm getting this kid home and bathed. Pretty sure she's got lots of stories to tell me tonight."

"After pizza. Which should—" he glanced at his watch "—be arriving in twenty minutes. With six dozen wings."

Libby couldn't remember the last time she'd splurged and ordered pizza, much less chicken wings.

"And while I was quite willing to pay

for it," he went on, "the volunteer fire department chief stopped by midday looking for some way to help you. He said your grandma would show up at every fire scene she could with food and drink for the firemen. He said it didn't matter how cold or wet or even snowy it was, Carolyn O'Laughlin would roll up to the site with a few other ladies and ladle out soup or pour coffee or hot chocolate or ice-cold sodas alongside trays of sandwiches and cookies. He said she never asked for a dime and would have refused if offered, and the department has never forgotten the true friend they have in the O'Laughlin family."

Her eyes filled with tears.

She'd refocused the drama with her mother onto what was best for Gramps. That had helped her back-burner that new twist in the road, but the story about Grandma's generous personality, her gracious nature, choked her up because Grandma had died thinking she'd failed Libby.

Nothing was further from the truth. If

anything, Libby had failed herself, but that was over now. She'd taken charge of her life and CeeCee's, and they were on a good road again.

But the thought of that kindly woman thinking she'd let Libby down stung, because Grandma had always put others first.

"I didn't meant to upset you." Concern formed a solid line between Jax's brows.

She swiped her eyes and shook her head. "You didn't. It's the story and knowing my grandma's selflessness. And just plain missing her because Grandma always knew what to do. I didn't always listen," she said softly. "But that woman could face any situation and see the ins and outs and put a plan in motion. She was the best example there could have been and I only wish I'd listened more carefully. Of course, if I had, I wouldn't have CeeCee, so maybe it's all part of God's plan."

CeeCee dashed across the restocked apple section just then, skidded to a stop and twirled. "I am going to wear my reddest red dress to church tomorrow because red is for apples and it's the best color ever for apple season," she announced. "Unless you're a green apple," she supposed then, eyeing the Granny Smith display. "So that means I'll wear green for those apples next week and then every apple will be so happy!"

Libby lifted the little girl up and kissed her sweet cheek. "It is impossible to worry too much when Miss Cecelia Creighton is around." She smiled right into Jax's eyes. "I'm taking this cute kid home and eating pizza. Will you make sure everyone's invited?"

"I sure will."

She carried CeeCee back to the truck. She didn't care that the girl was big enough to walk. She cared about precious moments with her child, watching her grow, helping her be the best person she could be.

Seeing her among the apples today didn't just spark a memory of another little girl over twenty years ago.

It ignited a tiny hope for what might be a future. A future for her grandparents' farm. If she could make enough money this season to fuel next year's production, she might be able to pull this off. Sure, she'd need to hire help, but with frugal spending and good oversight, maybe O'Laughlin Orchards wouldn't have to close.

"I loved being with all those people, Mommy." CeeCee laid her head against Libby's shoulder, then drew it right back up again. "But mostly I love being with you and my gramps and Mr. Jax and my teacher. Because you all love me so much!"

She hugged CeeCee before letting her climb onto the seat.

She'd messed up a lot of things, but not this child. Through the turbulence and bad times, she'd protected her daughter. CeeCee would grow up surrounded by love and cleanliness and wholesome apples. It couldn't get better than that.

But as she settled into the driver's seat, a different image appeared.

Jax's face. That smile. The memory of a kiss she couldn't erase.

He was kind and helpful and had jumped in with both feet to help. Was he a rare man or had her past left her jaded and untrusting?

Maybe both, she decided as she drove up the road. But being around Jax McClaren made her want to trust again. That could either be wonderfully good or a fool's option, and she was determined to never be fooled again.

Chapter Fourteen

Jax got to the apple barn early the next morning. Libby was taking Cleve and CeeCee to church, so he was a one-man crew to get things righted before they opened at eleven.

He could have gone with them. CeeCee had invited him and Cleve had promised to hold him a seat. Of course, he probably forgot that offer minutes after he made it, but the sincerity was there.

He rolled crates of apples out of the cooler and started bagging them. He usually tried to avoid mindless work that gave him too much time to think, but not today. Today it was just fine.

He whistled softly as he bagged. He hadn't bagged this many apples since he was a young boy. Kids didn't bag apples at CVF anymore. Robotic machines gently sorted, turned, washed, dried and crated the fruit into pressed paper packaging to avoid bruising. So different from its humble origins. But then, CVF was marketing internationally to hundreds of thousands of customers, the beauty of Washington Perfect fruit gracing tables around the world.

But this—

"Hey, farm boy, want some help?"

He turned, surprised to hear his brother Ken's voice. "Why aren't you at church? And yes, of course I do. I've got ninety minutes to get this place back into shape."

"I'm praying over here this morning. Dad said you guys did thousands of dollars yesterday. We figured some extra hands might be in order. We'll leave before the family gets back." He jutted his chin toward the back door as their younger brother, Andrew, came in. "How about we bag and you go fix the fall displays?"

Jax read between the lines. If someone drove by and recognized his brothers, Libby would hear of it.

"Sounds good." He moved out front and began restocking the pumpkins and gourds they'd unloaded the night before. He righted the huge display of cornstalks, and watered nearly two hundred mums. They'd sold over a hundred the previous day, and it felt good to see cars and SUVs stuffed with farm goods as they drove away.

So many happy people. Happy to buy apples and veggies and pumpkins. Happy with life as if being happy was a simple task.

It used to be.

The mental reminder nudged gently.

When you were helping Grandma Molly and tending baby trees and learning the art of grafting from your grandfather. You were at peace, then.

He was, he realized, but he realized something else, too. He'd never borne the weight of other people's demise on his shoulders then, so it was easy to be happy. To embrace life and feel good.

And this felt good now.

Handling produce, building displays, even interacting with the people yesterday, a role thrust on him because of Cleve's misfortune. He'd stayed out on the perimeters of life since coming home, but he not only enjoyed yesterday's role of interacting with customers—he'd loved it.

"Hey, we're heading out now, before someone spots us." Andrew jogged his way and barreled into him with a big hug, the kind that used to turn into a family room wrestling match. "This looks great, jerk."

"Moron." He noogied his brother's head good-naturedly. "Thanks for coming over. I needed the help."

"Duh." Andrew rolled his eyes. "Next time ask, why don't you? Making people guess isn't the best way to get things done. Don't be dumb."

"I won't. Mostly."

Andrew's words made him think as the men drove back toward Quincy.

He'd made people guess what was going on inside him, mostly because he wasn't sure what was going on himself. That was changing now.

He pulled out his phone and scrolled. His therapist had sent him the referral for the newly developed treatment.

He quickly called and left a voice mail for the Seattle-based practitioner. He wouldn't hear anything back on a Sunday, but that didn't matter. He'd made the move and that was what he needed to do.

CeeCee, Cleve and Libby arrived a few minutes later. Gert and her husband showed up with two dozen frosted cinnamon rolls from a popular Wenatchee bakery, and a pair of college girls rolled in at ten forty-five and donned apple-red aprons.

Libby motioned them over. "Samantha and Tori, right?"

The taller girl raised her hand. "Samantha."

"Which makes me Tori," said the shorter girl.

"And don't tell Mr. Moyer I said this, but this place looks amazing," Samantha continued. "It's like a dream country store!"

"Samantha and Tori used to work over at Moyer's apple stand near Wenatchee," Libby told Jax. "He told me how good they were, but I couldn't afford to hire them until we made some money. Now we have, thanks to you."

He didn't want credit for helping. "You grew the apples and you have the eye for this stuff. I just do what I'm told."

She laughed.

He loved hearing her laugh. He loved seeing her joy, and maybe someday she'd tell him about that scar along her left jaw.

Maybe she wouldn't, and that would be

all right, too. She told him that she refused to let her past govern her present.

Wise words.

Samantha and Tori handled the inside customers with Gert and CeeCee's help, he and Libby took care of the outside ones, and it took all of them to keep an eye on Cleve.

"He's in his element," noted Jax as Cleve explained which apples were best for pies and canning to a group of middle-aged women.

"The art of the sale is never lost on Gramps, but our barn never looked this fancy, even in its prime," Libby replied. "I loved being able to help with this, to see how it would be to grow a business up from the ground floor. I've got a slew of ideas for next year," she went on. "Wouldn't it be fun to grow my own pumpkins and gourds? And I bet I could grow mums, too, I'm good with that kind of thing. Then I don't have to remarket all of this, I can be the direct sale point. No middleman means better prices for customers and better profit margin for the farmer."

She was still thinking of staying in business on her own. Was she serious?

One look into her shining eyes said yes.

She'd managed to get through this first year, so maybe she could do it. Women in his family weren't afraid to work alongside the men, and Aunt Connie wielded as much Ingerson clout as any of her brothers. "That first section of trees should come down," he noted as he finished resetting the pumpkin display corner. "If those were taken down quickly, there'd be time to work that land up for produce next year. It's about a six-acre plot."

"That's a lot of pumpkins."

Her expression made him laugh. "It sure is. But I don't think you'll have any trouble selling them. Not from the looks of this weekend, despite this short break in the action."

"Something to think about. And plan for. And it looks like our little lull is over," she noted as three cars rolled into the gravel lot. They were immediately followed by two more.

He withdrew his phone and touched the screen. "Seattle just kicked off to LA. I expect we'll see our share of moms and kids this afternoon."

"Football?"

"Yes, ma'am."

Cleve came their way as the cars pulled in. He paused, greeted the customers, then rounded the cars. "We've got a lot of business going on today, don't we?"

"Sure do, Gramps. It's wonderful." Libby had been readjusting mums so the display looked fuller even though they'd sold dozens already. She paused and hugged his arm. "Like old times, huh?"

He grinned. "Just what we needed. Exactly what I hoped for. I couldn't be happier, Dianna."

Libby's face went flat. She started to open her mouth, then didn't, but she let go of his arm. "I'm going to check inside." She strode away with a quick gait.

"We've done good, haven't we?" Cleve grinned at Jax with the innocence of a child. "I told her mama that if we held on, she'd come around, and she did. She did, all right. Won't Carolyn be happy to see it?"

Jax held his tongue. Cleve thought Libby was his estranged daughter.

No wonder she walked away. The randomness of this wretched disease coaxed people to say and do things they'd never consider in their normal state, but a clogged brain was a dangerous thing. "Libby's been working really hard to put this together."

Cleve frowned.

He turned. Stared at the barn, then Jax, then up the road. "This isn't my place."

"You're using it this year because your place ran into some trouble with the wind. Mr. Moyer offered his barn to help you and Libby out."

"Libby." For a moment he almost looked lucid, but then he spotted CeeCee and grinned. "There's my little girl! How are you, darlin'?"

"I'm so very good, Gramps!" She skipped their way and Jax didn't know if Cleve was seeing CeeCee for herself or as her mother at the same age. In the end, he guessed it didn't much matter because the old fellow beamed with happiness.

"Can you help me sell apples?" CeeCee asked. She clutched her grandpa's big hand and swung it back and forth. "Because there are so many people who want to know about our apples and I'm almost out of words!"

Jax couldn't imagine CeeCee out of words, but Cleve moved forward. "I'm glad to help, and it seems like the Moyers have done mighty well for themselves over here. Mighty well. I really like what they've done with the place."

Jax's words hadn't penetrated. Cleve didn't quite get it, that these were *his* apples and *his* success. Or that Libby had worked so hard to help orchestrate the whole thing.

Jax greeted customers as they exited their cars. It was a classic autumn Sunday with cornstalks, pumpkins, apples and football.

But when he passed the open double doors, he took a moment to search out Libby. She was at the far end of the barn, working with a customer, but when she spotted Cleve at the other end, her look of sorrow cut Jax.

He understood there was little he could do. Grandma Molly didn't recognize anyone by the time she passed on, and each family member dealt with that in their own way. Some hadn't handled it all that well.

Dianna.

That was Libby's mother's name. He knew that because he saw it on the farm records. Not because it was spoken in the house.

As two more minivans pulled in, followed by a short string of SUVs, he put thoughts of old discord behind him because no matter how Cleve phrased it, this was Libby's success. For today, apples and pumpkins took center stage, and like CeeCee said, it was easy to be happy around so many happy people. And that part of this felt downright good.

Ten thousand four-hundred dollars went into the bank on Monday morning, and when Libby exited the Golden Grove Bank & Trust, her feet felt light.

There was money in the bank.

She hadn't had a positive account balance that wasn't needed for bills in years. Depending on the fall weather, there were at least four weeks of significant sales time remaining. Maybe more if the weather held and she stayed open until Thanksgiving. Would all the weekends be this busy?

Maybe not, this had been a record breaker but even more important than the money was the look of sheer pleasure on Gramps's face yesterday.

He'd called her Dianna. She thought of that as she opened the truck door.

He'd never made that mistake before.

Was it because Libby's mother had come to see him in the hospital? Did he even realize she was there? She'd left before he woke up, but maybe he sensed her presence. Or was his brain just getting more tied up in knots as the days went on?

Her phone rang. She spotted the school's phone number and answered quickly. "Hi, Libby Creighton here."

"Ms. Creighton, this is Sandy Wilburn, I'm the school coordinator for Golden Grove Elementary."

"Yes?"

"It seems we had several students out at your farm this past weekend and they loved it. CeeCee's teacher was wondering if we could make a field trip to the farm in the next week or two. We'd bring the kids by bus, and maybe you could show them an orchard, talk to them about apples and fruits and farming. And then a visit to the sales barn would be lovely, so they can get an idea of what a farmer does, how they grow the food, then sell it. Some kids have no idea how food is produced and we'd love to give them that experience."

Libby didn't hesitate. "We'd be delighted to do that. And I can order some donuts to have on hand for snack time. We don't produce anything like that yet, but we've got everything else."

The coordinator's sigh sounded happy. "Donuts and apples sound wonderful! I'll email you possible dates that buses are available. If you could get right back to me about which works best for you, I'll reserve the bus and the drivers. I'm so glad you're able to accommodate us."

The thought of CeeCee's classmates seeing all this should put their talk of homelessness to rest. "We're happy to do so," she replied. "I'll watch for that email."

"Perfect."

She got back to the house just as Mortie was finishing up her visit with Gramps. Libby tucked a bottle of milk and a pack of Gramps's favorite hot dogs into the fridge.

She met Mortie as she crossed toward the kitchen. "How's he doing?"

Mortie made a face. "He's doing all right, considering. His little adventure wore him out more than he thought."

"Plus our busy Sunday," offered Libby.

Mortie shrugged that off. "Seeing all those people was the best medicine for him. The weather's nice, and he's an outdoorsman. Always has been. I'd stick to your plan of having him at the apple stand with you. You wanted to give him a great season, Libby, and you're doing it." She tugged on a lightweight jacket. "You got to the bank all right?"

"With more money than I've ever held in my life," Libby whispered. "I kept telling myself to walk natural. Be casual. Pretend you're not carrying around a pouch full of money."

Mortie laughed softly. "It's an odd feeling, for sure, especially these days of automatic deposits and withdrawals. I never thought I'd see the day when cash was the exception to the rule. I'm going on to my next call. I saw Jax and a couple of people going into the orchard to pick just a few minutes back."

"Thank you, Mortie."

"And about Courtney," Mortie asked. "Are you all right having her work here or would you prefer someone else?"

Libby had considered that question and she'd come to the conclusion that no one was at sole fault for Gramps's disappearing act. If she was going to keep Gramps at home like she promised, she had to be strong enough to take responsibility for whatever happened. Courtney hadn't been negligent, and the new locks would help keep Gramps from slipping out unnoticed again. "I will welcome her back. She's good with him, and the new locks should help keep him out of danger. And honestly, I appreciate the help she's willing to give, so yes. Tell her we understand."

"Good. That will be a relief to her."

She waved goodbye as her grandfather

came out of his room. "Gramps, I'm going to have you go up the road with me to the apple shop, okay? If you don't mind working for a living, that is," she added, teasing.

"Can't abide sittin' around doing nothing. Lollygaggin'." He frowned. "Up the road, you say?"

"To Moyer's barn. We're using it this year."

"That wind was a fierce thing, wasn't it?" He said the words as if remembering was suddenly the norm again. "It almost blew me away with that barn."

Her heart thumped. The image of Gramps outside, alone, with the barn being blown to smithereens made her realize how close things came to an even greater disaster that day.

"All I could think of was getting that tractor under cover before something bad happened. And I did it."

"You did." She didn't tell him that his action compounded their loss by a good twenty-thousand dollars. "Thank you for looking out for us, Gramps."

"Well, I promised your mama a long time ago, and I don't make a promise and then not keep it. O'Laughlins say what they mean and mean what they say."

She didn't know if he meant Grandma or Dianna, but it really didn't matter. She patted his arm gently. "That's a great quality to pass on, isn't it?"

He smiled as he went outside, and when he spotted Jax driving out of the orchard with a full bed of apples, Cleve's smile deepened. He moved toward Jax, grinning at the sight of freshly picked fruit. "Now, that's a good start to the day right there," he exclaimed. "Nice job, young man."

Jax accepted the compliment with his customary grace. "Thank you, sir. I had help. The guys are working on the last of the pears. We'll have them all in the cooler by tonight, but I figured we'd want to restock the hardest-hit apple varieties from over the weekend, so we focused on that first."

"Smart thinking. I'm going out with this young lady right now. I'll be back in a bit and I'll settle accounts then."

Jax didn't blink an eye. "Sounds good, sir." He helped Gramps into the passenger seat of the truck with gentle, firm hands while Libby scanned the apple crates. He must have started at first light to have that many apples picked, and light didn't come any too early this time of year. Another act of kindness or just good business sense?

She started toward the old pickup. Jax rounded the hood and beat her to the door, and when he opened it for her...

When his eyes met hers—

Her heart jumped again.

It didn't just pick up the pace. It soared. And when he gently closed the door for her, the mix of strength and compassion tugged her emotions.

Her phone pinged, indicating she had

an email. She opened it before she pulled away, then showed him the email exchange. "CeeCee's school would like to bring the kindergarten classes here for a field trip next week and I'm going to need someone else here whichever day we pick."

"Any day works for me." He lowered his voice deliberately. "I'll make sure Cleve's safe and sound. That's what's concerning you, right?"

"If I'm distracted by sixty five-year-olds, I'm afraid I'd lose track of him," she whispered. "I don't dare do that."

"No problem, ma'am. I'll be on hand."

"Thank you."

He winked.

That put her heart back into overdrive, but the minute he did it, she smiled, encouraging more winks. Because when Jax winked at her, she wasn't the ragamuffin girl or the cast-off wife any longer.

She was the successful young farmer with a bright future ahead of her. And that wasn't just the money in the bank talking.

That was the smile of a good, kind man who made her feel like she was something special.

And Libby hadn't felt special in a long time.

Chapter Fifteen

Jax followed them to the apple barn. He unloaded some of the crates into the cooler, and others onto the sales floor for bagging. When Cleve seemed comfortable bagging the fruit, Jax let himself relax a little. Weekdays didn't have the Saturday and Sunday crush of customers, but Libby was on her own today, and Cleve liked to keep busy. Jax didn't want the old fellow to go wandering when Libby was taking care of customers, but as long as he was working, Cleve seemed to maintain focus.

His brother Ken texted him as he drove

back to the orchard an hour later. I'm at the Quincy office. Come straight over.

Can't, he texted back. Picking apples, and the engineers are coming to stake out the Creighton barn.

You might want to reconsider putting all that money into a barn, Ken wrote back. Come over now. Cleve O'Laughlin just sold the farm to CVF with a signed contract dated in August. This isn't how any of us saw this going down.

Cleve sold the farm?

He couldn't have. If he had, they'd have known about it, but Libby did say that a CVF representative had come calling last year. Then Ken had followed up.

It couldn't be right. Somehow, something had gotten messed up because Cleve was one hundred percent determined to keep the farm out of corporate hands.

Ken's message left him no choice but to drive over to the company headquarters on the far side of Quincy and see what was going on. But first he had to make sure everything was set up for the day.

He phoned the hired pickers and squared things with them. He met Gert and the other drivers as they pulled into the farm and explained what was needed.

Gert was loading up apple bags while he talked. She handed them out and hooked her thumb toward the trees. "Are crates set?"

"Did that first thing. And Dave's got his truck here if you need to take apples up the road."

"Then we're good." She pulled a hat onto her head. Today's breeze spoke more of fall than summer. "We'll get on, then. You do what you need to do. We've got this."

He knew they did.

A part of him wanted to ask why. Why would regular folks give up hours of free time each day to help an old farmer?

There wasn't time to pose the question. The drivers strode toward the orchard at a quick pace, anxious to work. He climbed into his truck and drove east. All the way there, he tried to make sense of Ken's words.

He couldn't.

First, Cleve had made his feelings quite clear about selling. And he'd been training Libby on fruit husbandry for over a year. Why do that if he intended to sell?

He couldn't think about what this might do to Libby. She'd been so excited about banking money from her very first harvest.

Ken had to be wrong, and yet his brother prided himself on never being wrong.

He drove to Quincy, conflicted. He wasn't sure how this had happened, or how to fix it, but the one thing he knew was that there was no way on earth to explain this to Libby. And he didn't even want to try.

Cleve O'Laughlin's signature was scrawled across every page of the contract that CVF had offered midsummer, and the pages not requiring a signature had been initialed. That meant the person signing understood old legalities enough to make sure their intention was known.

But how?

Why?

"This is a major problem, Jax." He father scowled at the paperwork, scrubbed a hand across his fairly bald head and scowled some more. "How did this happen?"

"I have no idea. He's been saying all along that he's signing the farm over to Libby and he's been encouraging her to do all she can to make it a success. When he's cognizant enough to think clearly, that is."

"Can we nullify the contract?" wondered Ken. "We could cite his cognitive decline and renege on the offer."

"I can guarantee he's not in control of his faculties to make this decision and I sincerely doubt that he was that much better midsummer."

"Does his granddaughter want him to sell?" asked Jax's father. "Is it possible that they came up with this as a solution to money problems? Maybe he wants to leave her money instead of property?"

"Nothing she's said would indicate that," Jax replied. He reread the contract CVF had drawn up midsummer. "You allowed a three-month window on this contract, so he's gotten it in with two weeks to spare."

He scowled as he scanned the forms again. Why had Cleve signed them? And why hadn't he let Libby know? Was it a forgotten detail? And yet, he hadn't mailed the papers until now.

It made no sense. He stared at the papers and one thought came to mind: Libby's joy over the busy apple sales, the happy people, the bustling store, the pinnacle of her year of hard work. "We have to break the contract."

Ken made a face. "We can cite his diminished capacity, of course, but it's a delicate situation. No one wants to make his condition worse. If he signed this over the summer—"

"Sat on it—" mused Richard.

"Then sent it off a few days ago, what's

changed?" asked Ken. "What's gotten him to do this? The accident in the creek?"

Jax didn't know. "He came home from the hospital on Saturday. He must have put this right in the mailbox for the postal worker to pick up when he got home."

"You've got to fix this, son." Richard steepled his hands. "Whichever way it goes is fine with us. We didn't put an offer on the land randomly. We wanted it. But I'm not putting a mother and child and an old man out of their home and livelihood because he might have had a bad day. You said he was happy with how busy it was yesterday at the farm stand, correct?"

"Ecstatic. In his lucid moments anyway. So how can we take this at face value when we know those lucid moments are rare?"

"Murky waters," his father said. "If he'd given Libby power of attorney, we'd have that legal recourse, but if he hasn't it's tougher."

"Unless we pretend it didn't arrive," said Ken.

Richard frowned. "We can't do that.

We're honest people. We have to work this out for everyone's well-being. And to respect an old man's wishes. I can keep a lid on this for a little while, but, Jax, you've got to talk to his granddaughter. See what she thinks. And if Mr. O'Laughlin hasn't drawn up a will yet, someone should make sure he does. Soon."

A will.

A sold farm.

Libby's hopes and dreams and plans for the future whisked out from under her.

There was no way Jax could let that happen. "I'll talk to her. See if she has any idea what's going on. And I'll talk to Cleve, too, because none of this makes any sense."

"Jax." His father rounded the desk and crossed the small room. Richard Ingerson wasn't the kind of guy who wasted production space on lavish offices, a quality he carried through life. "Do they know who you are?"

"They do not." He gripped the folder he clutched a little tighter. "But they will now."

He didn't wait to see his brother's expression of regret or his dad's sympathy. There was a job to be done and his army training clicked in. When there was a job to do, send in your best men to do it. Today—in Golden Grove—he was the best man for the job. He didn't have to like it, but he had to do it.

He got into his truck, grabbed a coffee from a convenience store on Route 28 and drove north, knowing that each mile was bringing him closer to shattering someone's hopes and dreams. The fact that they were Libby's dreams only made the trip that much harder.

Libby spotted Jax coming out of the orchard around five thirty and met him when he parked the truck. "We made over a thousand dollars today. On a Monday, Jax. That's amazing, isn't it?"

He smiled, but the expression seemed forced today. Not normal for the guy who'd worked so hard to make sure this all worked out. "That's a solid day, for sure."

"And thank you for grabbing CeeCee off the bus and bringing her over. We had a little quiet time and she did her reading. Was Gramps okay for you?"

"Fine. Quiet, kind of. Courtney came and got him settled, so I went out to work."

"And they staked out the barn." She pointed to the neon-flagged ground stakes, marking the barn's new footprint and buried utilities. "Thank you for overseeing all of that. There's no way I could do this without you, and I'm truly grateful."

Her words made him wince. "Libby, I—"

"Mom, I am so hungry and it's suppertime, right?" CeeCee dashed out the side door. It banged shut behind her. She stopped, glanced over her shoulder with an "oops" look, then raced forward again. "Is it hot dogs? Please say it's hot dogs!"

"I got them this morning because you and Gramps love them. CeeCee, you've been such a big help to me on the farm," she said, looping her arm around the girl's shoulders. "And I'm so proud of how well you're doing in school. Girl, you're reading already. That's amazing!"

"It sure is." Jax tipped a full-fledged smile down at CeeCee, then bumped knuckles with her. "Great job."

"Well, it's so easy," the five-year-old bragged. "And sometimes I help Henry and Dottie with their work because I know how to make every single letter both ways and I can almost always color in all the lines. Except some of the tiny ones and they're just silly," she added.

"Thank you for helping others, CeeCee. That's a wonderful thing. Let's get you and Gramps fed and then we'll have some story time."

"I'll pick the books!" She ran back into the house, and caught the wooden door just before it banged shut.

"Good job," Libby called out.

CeeCee's grin was enough of an answer in the fading light. She shifted her attention back to Jax. "It's getting dark ear-lier now, and I know that's expected, but there's not much time to get back here and do anything in the evening except supper, dishes and reading. You were about to ask me something?" she added as she moved toward the house. He opened the screen door and let her precede him, a gentleman's gesture.

"We need a time to talk. I've got some-thing I have to go over with you."

The barn, she assumed, and she was about to reply when Cleve met them in the kitchen. He had the truck keys in his hand and a determined expression. "I'm head-ing into town. The diner's got meat loaf on Wednesdays and we always go for the meat loaf special on Wednesdays. I guess your grandma's meeting me there."

His nighttime confusion was growing worse with the diminishing light. The shorter days seemed to exacerbate his sun-downing, and that could mean a long, tough winter ahead.

"Gramps, that would be such a nice treat." Libby treated his confusion like it was no big deal as Jax quietly shut the door. "Except it's Monday and the diner's closed on Monday. We'll put meat loaf on hold for a couple of days, all right?"

"Monday?" He squinted at the apple-themed wall calendar. "You sure?"

"Absolutely, and we had a good opening weekend, so I got your favorite hot dogs this morning, and some of those soft rolls you like so much."

"With the yellow mustard?" The gruff note of his voice suggested that hot dogs couldn't quite replace the meat loaf he had his heart set on.

"The yellowest."

Just a few months ago, he'd have shrugged off the change and been delighted that she'd gotten one of his favorites.

Not today.

Chin down, he trudged back to the living room and sank into his recliner like a small child denied a treat.

"How can I help?"

Jax's voice made her turn. "Have hot dogs with us. Pretend things are normal, because I'm going to be honest. I love how busy the apple stand is, but between Gramps and—" she paused a moment to choke back emotion before she went on "—his decline, I'm drained. I'd love some grown-up support tonight. If you don't mind? And what did you want to talk about?" she asked as she slung her sweater onto a short rack of hooks hanging inside the kitchen door.

"Nothing we have to discuss tonight," he told her. "We'll tackle it tomorrow."

"Good." She sent him a tired smile. "Because the last thing I want to do is upset his applecart any more than it already is." She angled a look toward the living room. "When he's like this, the best thing to do is lie low for a bit."

"Grandma Molly was the same way. Can I fire up the grill on the back porch?"

"Yes, thanks." She tried to hide her excitement, because Gramps had an old-fashioned charcoal grill. Taking the time to get it started and let coals form was way too long. "He loves hot dogs on the grill. Thank you, Jax."

He grabbed a pack of matches and crossed to the door. "My pleasure, ma'am."

Strong. Kind. Honest. A man of valor.

She'd promised herself to steer clear of men and romance for a good reason, but reason flew out the window whenever Jax walked through the door. Maybe she'd walled herself up too much after a really bad experience. She wasn't a foolish nineteen-year-old anymore. She'd grown up these past seven years, and she was no moonstruck girl falling for pretty words. She was a woman, able to appreciate a good man when she found one.

So maybe she was wrong to set such firm

borders because when she was around Jax McClaren, borders were the last thing on her mind.

Chapter Sixteen

Jax didn't doze off early enough for his sleep to be interrupted by nightmares that night. Guilt kept him awake. His last glimpse of the clock said 2:05 a.m., so the six o'clock alarm was a rude awakening. But not as gut-wrenching as what Libby was going to experience today, so he cleaned up, shaved and made coffee. Then headed downhill to confront Libby with his father's news.

Would she even talk with him once she discovered his identity? Would she want him around?

Especially when she realized her farm might have been sold out from under her.

He pulled in just before the morning bus came. CeeCee waited until he parked the truck, then tossed her backpack to the ground and raced his way. "Good morning, Mr. Jax! Isn't it a beautiful day? Like, the best day ever?"

He'd give anything to see things through her eyes right now. "I can't deny it," he told her as he hoisted her up. "Are you ready to go to school and help your friends Denry and Hottie?"

She burst out laughing as she corrected him. "Henry and Dottie! You're so funny, Mr. Jax. I love you!"

Then she reached over and hugged him, right before she gave him a big kiss on the cheek. She held on to him as if he were important, and for those few seconds, he felt like he was.

"Bus is coming," called Libby.

"Yikes!" CeeCee grinned at him, scrambled down, grabbed her backpack and slung it over her shoulders like an old pro. "See you later, guys!" She waved as she hurried toward the road, quite comfortable with this new normal. "Have a great day on the farm!"

"You have a great day in school," Libby answered. She waved to CeeCee and Gert, then waved to the kids in the window seats. Most of the older kids acted too cool to respond, but a few of the younger ones waved avidly.

As the bus pulled away, she turned toward him. "Well, you got an enthusiastic greeting this morning. And a kiss."

Two things he probably didn't deserve, but CeeCee had no idea about that. Neither did her sweet mother. "She's an amazing kid, Libby."

"She is, isn't she? And I'm blessed to be her mom. To have the chance to do all this for her, despite the past. To see her go off like that, so happy and well-adjusted, and to see how excited she was when some of her classmates showed up at the apple store this past weekend." Remembering the kids' positive reaction deepened her smile. "It was amazing to see the change in their attitudes from kids who thought we were homeless a few weeks ago, to kids who realized that CeeCee has a pretty amazing life here."

"Why would they think you were homeless?" he asked.

She drew a deep breath as the two pickers drove in and parked. They needed no direction today. They waved and headed straight for the newer section of apples.

"Because we *were* homeless," she admitted. "When CeeCee's father took off, he emptied our accounts. I was working, but there was no way I could afford rent, food, gas and to pay off the bills he left behind. The cost of living in the Seattle area is steep. CeeCee talked about that at school, so some of the kids thought she didn't have a place to live."

She'd been homeless and struggling for food. Other than a few occasions on active duty, he'd never had to miss a meal in his life. An urge to care for her, to care for both of them surged over him, and yet he was here to mess up her newfound security. The image of them struggling made him cringe. "I'm sorry you went through that. I had no idea."

"At that same time Grandma called me with her prognosis and said they needed help." She paused for a moment, taking a breath. "She didn't know we were homeless. She thought I was ashamed of them and that's why I didn't drive back here to see them. The truth was that I stayed gone because I was ashamed of my choices. My life. Skillful abusers excel at cutting people off from those who love them, and making you feel isolated, abandoned. But when things got rough for her and Gramps, she called because she always believed that family should stick together, and I'm so glad she did that. It gave CeeCee and me a home, and I was able to help Grandma through her illness. Now we'll do the same for Gramps, although it's going to be hard on CeeCee. How does a five-year-old deal with two deaths so close together?"

"It's tough," he told her. "I was seven when we lost my mother. My grandmother raised me and my brothers while Dad worked. For a long time I hated to get up every day, knowing I'd never see my mom again. To this day I'm thankful for Grandma Molly's sacrifice. She stepped in and loved us all. I don't know what we would have done without her."

She touched his arm in sympathy. "That's why you're so understanding. I decided that the best example I can set for CeeCee is to be loving and giving in times of hardship. If I live my life that way, she'll learn it instinctively. Sometimes life lessons are the best teachers and I learned that from my grandmother."

She'd been through so much the past few years. How could he put her through more? And yet, he had no choice. He jutted his chin toward the house. "Is Cleve awake?"

She nodded. "For hours. And thank you for those locks or he'd have been wandering at five o'clock this morning. He couldn't figure out how to get the door open, and finally he grumbled something about the trees and went back to bed."

"He doesn't think to look down, but if he spots CeeCee doing it, he might figure it out."

"I reminded her of that this morning." She tapped the side door as they went inside. "This door is out of sight from his chair, and the front door is a keyed dead bolt and Gramps doesn't have the key. So far, so good. What do we need to discuss?" she continued. She motioned outside. "Something to do with the barn?"

He only wished it was that easy. "No. Let's talk in the kitchen so we can hear Cleve if he needs us."

"And have coffee." She shot him an over-the-shoulder smile that spiked his heart rhythm, but he knew the smile would be short-lived and there was nothing he could do about that. He went into the living room to greet Cleve while she fixed her coffee. She brought it to the table as he reentered the kitchen a few minutes later. "You sure you don't want any?" she asked.

"I'm sure. But thank you." He hooked his thumb toward the living room. "Cleve's watching a nature show on cable."

"He loves those things. He'll find one thing extremely intriguing and focus on it, then follow me around to tell me about it dozens of times."

He remembered his grandmother's repetitive stories. "Like a video stuck on replay."

"Yes." She took a seat. "So what's going on?"

His heart sped up. His hands grew damp, but he took a seat opposite her and set the folder on the table. "A few things, and I have to preface this by being honest with you. Honest about who I am and why I'm here. My name isn't just Jax McClaren, Libby." He drew a deep breath, swiped his palms against his jeans, and waded in. "It's

Jackson McClaren *Ingerson*, and I'm part of CVF. And in this folder is a contract that Cleve signed and dated in August, agreeing to sell O'Laughlin Orchards to CVF. It arrived on my father's desk yesterday and we have to figure out some way to fix this, Libby. Hopefully together."

Her heart literally stopped beating.

She couldn't have heard him correctly, and yet, he sat there, looking so utterly sincere, confessing he'd been living a lie these past weeks. Her tongue didn't want to obey her brain and it took her long seconds before she could wrap her head around his statement. "You're an Ingerson."

"Yes."

"And you just happened to come along one day and there was an old man out wandering the road—"

"You know that. Yes."

"And you just *happened* to stop and then ingratiate yourself to my family and friends…"

"Libby, it wasn't like that," he began, but she held up a hand for him to stop.

"Don't. Don't sit there and tell me what it was or wasn't like because you've been dishonest from the beginning. There's no way in the world I'm going to believe anything you say now." Cold chills ran up her spine and down her arms.

He'd lied to her. All this time. After she promised herself she'd never let another man fool her.

She'd let him into the house, into their lives, into their affections, and he'd played her every step of the way. Hadn't she just prided herself on being more astute, more mature?

How could one intelligent woman be so gullible? Was she that needy for someone to love her?

Her heart broke. It didn't just break in half, it shattered into a million frozen pieces because she'd promised herself to remain aloof, then fell for another con man. *Well, add it to the list, sugar.*

That was what her brain said. Her heart was too dumbstruck to say a thing.

"We have to fix this," he told her. He opened the folder on the table. "My father and brother met with me yesterday when they received this. Look at it, Libby." He handed her the top two forms. "It's the land sale contract they left here midsummer. It's signed and dated in early August. I don't know why Cleve would throw our representative out on his ear one minute, then sign the agreement and shelve it, but we had to tell you about it."

She stood up.

She couldn't sit there and casually drink coffee while he was about to acquire a beautiful piece of O'Laughlin family history that she'd always assumed would be hers.

He stood, too. "Listen, my father's a good man."

At this moment, she didn't care. "He might be, but he's also a businessman, and he's been wanting this farm for years, according to Grandma. Congratulations, Jackson." She folded her arms over her chest to fight off the tears that threatened to take over. "You've done it. I don't know how you managed it, but you did and I'm not about to put a sick old man through the wringer to fight you on it, and I expect you knew that."

"Libby, don't—"

"Go."

He started to come around the table. "It wasn't like that. None of it. I—"

"Please stop." She kept her arms folded, but she met his gaze head-on because she'd been put through the wringer once. It wasn't going to happen again. "I can't possibly believe all these things happened by chance. That you happened to be driving by at the very moment the barn blew down and Gramps was walking down the road and there you were, all knight-in-shining-armor friendly, ready to jump in and help with everything. And you did it so smoothly that I'm relatively certain you've had lots of practice because the odds against something like this are beyond astronomical. So, go. Leave me a copy of your signed contract and I'll make sure that everything is in order before we move out. Do we have time to finish the selling season, or would you prefer that we leave the income potential for you, too?"

"I was just coming out for another cuppa because that first one was so good." Cleve strolled into the kitchen right then and he beamed at one, then the other. "My Carolyn enjoyed having coffee with me in this kitchen. It does my heart good to see you young ones doing the same. This room's held a lot of love over the years." He smiled, sighed and crossed to the coffee pot. "It's got space for more, I reckon."

His sweet remembrance only made this moment tougher, because she'd let herself dream again. That made her feel even more foolish.

"I'll get to work." Jax had taken off the faded army cap when he came in. He tugged it back into place and headed for the side door.

"Not here," she called after him. "We're fine here on our own. Just as we've always been."

He stopped. Would he turn around? Apologize? Tell her it was all a grand mistake?

He did no such thing.

He stood there for several drawn-out seconds. Then he squared his shoulders and went down the short flight of stairs to the door. And when that screen door slapped shut behind him, Libby was pretty sure that was the last she'd ever see of Jackson Mc-Claren... No, Jackson McClaren *Ingerson.* At least until she was forced to hand over the keys to the place her family had called home for over a hundred years. Gone—just like that. And there was no one to blame for any of this but herself.

Chapter Seventeen

Cheated.

Double-crossed.

And abandoned. Again.

Libby stared at the to-do list she'd made Thursday night. She'd crafted the optimistic list before CeeCee woke with a nightmare and before Gramps decided to save someone's baby from falling around 2:00 a.m. Of course, there was no baby and when she tried to tell him that, he stared at her—disbelieving, caught in whatever late-night image held him in its grip.

Dear God, help me do this. Help me,

please, because my low-fuel light's been on for days.

She'd spent the last three days running on minimal sleep and high-powered caffeine. There were still a lot of late-season apples to pick, sort and bag, orders to be filled, and the store and house to be maintained on top of watching over Gramps and CeeCee, but she was only one person. How could she possibly do it all?

She couldn't.

And yet there was little choice in the matter. *Come on. You can do anything for six weeks. Right?*

She wanted to believe that, but if something happened to Gramps or CeeCee during that time, how would she live with herself? Were apples all that important? Was anything all that important? And if the farm changed hands at the end of the season, at least she'd have the sale price in the bank.

Or will you?

She stopped looking at the list and re-considered what was going on around her.

She'd thought Gramps was leaving the farm to her until Jax came around waving a bill of sale. Did she dare count on the proceeds from the farm sale? Gramps and Grandma had drawn up a will leaving everything to her, but what if he'd changed that? It was his right to do so, but she needed to know what to expect, and when she went looking for a copy of the will, she couldn't find it.

And if Gramps needed costly end-of-life care, that would eat up the sale money, wouldn't it?

What if she did all this and there was nothing for her or CeeCee at the end? How would they live? Would they be forced back into homelessness? Gramps would never mean for that to happen under normal circumstances, but these were anything but normal.

Her head hurt.

She popped two pain pills, and poured a third cup of coffee as Mortie let herself in through the side door. Mortie stopped short on the top step and offered a frank assessment. "You have looked better, darlin'."

Libby groaned. "You're supposed to pretend you don't notice it, Mortie. What kind of friend are you?"

"The kind who tells the truth and, girl, you need sleep. And a moment to relax, but telling an apple farmer to relax in October is a fool's endeavor, for certain. How's Cleve this morning?"

"Restless." She explained about the broken sleep and Mortie winced in sympathy.

"I don't know what it is about babies, but this is a common thing in some of my later-stage patients. Worrying about them, seeing them, hearing them cry. What a wretched thing for a brain to do to an old person. I am praying for a cure for this disease so this will be the last generation we have fighting it. There is little dignity in growing old this way."

"I'll join you in that prayer," Libby told her. Then she handed Mortie an envelope.

"I can't get to town today and I want to get this over to CVF quickly. Can you drop it by the post office when you go through?"

Mortie studied the envelope. "Of course, but why are you writing to CVF? Were they here bothering Cleve again?"

"No." Libby hadn't found the nerve to openly discuss this latest development, but she had to now. Mortie would need to know because anything that affected Cleve could affect his care. "They haven't been back, but it seems that he decided to sell them the farm back in August and just mailed them the signed contract last Saturday when he came home from the hospital."

"He what?" Mortie stared at her, dumb-struck. She gripped the back of the kitchen chair so hard that her knuckles strained pale against her darker skin. "Cleve O'Laughlin would never sell this place to CVF and he would certainly not sell it out from under his own granddaughter. That's impossible, Libby."

How she wished that was the case, but

it wasn't. Libby made a face of regret. "It seems we're both wrong. Anyway, the whole thing blew up on Tuesday. I found out that Jax is really an Ingerson and he brought the signed real estate deal over to show me."

"Oh my."

Libby was pouring cream into her coffee. The note in Mortie's voice brought her chin up. "You're not surprised by that last part."

"No." Mortie frowned. "I knew who he was but I also knew why he was keeping it to himself. Your grandfather had been so adamant about not wanting to sell, and I know that Jax hasn't been working in the family business since he came home from the Middle East. I figured he'd tell you on his terms and in his own time. He's a good man and it wasn't up to me to call him out. Not when he was working so hard to keep this place going for you."

So Mortie was falling for this whole charade, too? That was another surprise. "You don't think it was odd that he showed up right when everything started falling apart?"

"Not when I'm a firm believer in God's timing," Mortie replied. "Some might call it a coincidence, but to put a trained apple producer who also has handyman skills and experience with dementia patients right here, at the best possible time? Totally a God thing. Isn't it?"

Libby was about to sip her coffee.

She didn't. She set it down and faced Mortie. "That's silly. It was clearly a setup to make sure they got the land."

"You said Cleve signed it over the summer, though."

"In early August. But—"

Mortie put both hands to her face and groaned softly. "I believe I know what happened and I'm afraid it's partly my fault." She pulled out her phone and scrolled for her online calendar. "August first, when you had CeeCee's school physical, I drove your grandfather into town for his checkup like we planned."

"And we all met back here for lunch."

"Yes, but the doctor's office was busy and they had Cleve waiting in a room. You know how he is about privacy with the doctor."

Libby knew, all right. Gramps would talk to the doctor, then the doctor would talk to Libby in a separate room.

"I'd already spoken with the nurse practitioner. I told them I was going across to the diner to get coffee and do some notes. They were going to let me know when Cleve was done, and they did, but when I went back there to get him, I saw your mother come out of the Market Street entrance and get into a car."

Her mother in Golden Grove midsummer? Surprise number three. "Did Gramps see her?"

Mortie sank into a chair. "I don't know. I didn't ask because I didn't want to upset him. I talked with Dr. Green, then got Cleve back home. He didn't say anything about it, and he'd already asked me to contact her if he got real bad. But why would he suddenly turn around and sign those papers the very next day? Would it have anything to do with your mother being in Golden Grove?"

"I don't know. It's so hard to know what might trigger reactions in Gramps now. You think he might have seen her?"

Mortie shrugged. "They were in the same area and he was in the waiting room when I came back for him, so it's possible. He was agitated that he was done and didn't have a ride. He said he didn't like to be ignored and I thought he was just annoyed with me for going across the street. So maybe he saw her? Maybe that triggered his agitation? You know how this is now. Almost anything can do it."

"But to come home and sell the farm?" The lack of rationale confounded Libby. "That's major. It took thought and follow-through. He might have been a little better in August than he is now, but he wasn't mindful enough to do that. Was he?"

"Oh, honey, if I could explain the workings of a dementia patient's mind, I'd be a rare bird," said Mortie. "The confusion comes and goes and messes fact and illusion on a regular basis. But of course he can't be held accountable for what he might have done in a fugue state."

Jax had said the same thing and she'd brushed him off. Coming from Mortie, with a few days to calm down, the lack of cognition defense gleamed brighter. "You really think so, Mortie?"

"Libby, I know so. I've been caring for troubled patients for a lot of years. I wish we could have gotten your grandfather to sign over power of attorney to you, but he's a stubborn old goat about that stuff. Even so, I will protest anything he signed for the past six months. He has not had the mental capacity to make consequential judgments in a long, long time. Case closed."

Libby hugged her. "I love you, Mortie. I don't know how I would have gotten through this far without you."

Mortie returned the hug. "The feelin' is

mutual, darlin'. And don't you be too hard on that nice young man who came along to help, managed to save Cleve's life twice and arranged to have everything fixed up after a disaster." Mortie ticked the list off on her fingers as she spoke. "I'd say he's a pretty upstanding fellow myself."

Mortie made a good point. Jax had done a lot of things to help them, but he'd been living a lie the whole time and she'd been down that rabbit trail before. Once was enough. "When you've been lied to all your life, you get sensitized. I promised myself that I was going to live a pristine life with CeeCee," she went on as she tucked the work list into her back pocket. "That I'd never fall for a deceitful person again. And then I did. If I can't trust my own judgment with men, how can I be a good mother to my daughter?" she asked honestly. "Children deserve to have the best possible parents. It didn't happen for me, but I'm going to make sure it happens for my little girl."

"I can't argue with that." Mortie crossed

to the sink and washed her hands. "You go on about your morning. I've got this. I can drive Cleve over to the barn once I've taken care of him."

"Thanks, Mortie. There's a ton to do before we hit the ground running for this weekend. I'll see you later." She tugged a hoodie on as she passed the row of hooks inside the door. The morning had a late-season briskness that brought those final fruits to full sugar. Sunny days and crisp, cold nights were perfect for finishing apples. She drove her small hatchback to the barn. The pickers would load crates of apples onto the farm pickup and drive them over later. For now she'd restock what she could and get areas ready for the Braeburns and the Pinks, two local favorites.

She parked the car and walked inside the barn shortly after nine o'clock. She had an hour to restock and straighten up, so she flicked the lights on, closed the door and turned.

The apples were filled.

The displays were, too. Backup stock had been set out where needed, the cider coolers were full and bags of white, orange and striped miniature pumpkins filled an entire display table that had been left pretty empty yesterday. The apple display tables had been readjusted, leaving space for the Braeburns and the Pinks, just now ready to come to the store.

Jax.

It had to be him, he was the only person who had access to the barn. She'd forgotten to get that extra key back when she'd asked him to leave on Tuesday.

Her heartbeat revved up. She looked around and realized that he'd saved her hours of hands-on work, hours she didn't have.

Was he trying to ingratiate himself still? Or was he just a nice guy, like Mortie intimated? How could she know for sure?

You could try talking to him.

She considered that fairly obvious option as she unpacked the back of her car. Grandma had stored totes of vintage Thanksgiving things in the farmhouse basement. Turkey collectibles, rustic wooden wall art and pumpkin-shaped candleholders had been tucked into the large plastic containers with a collection of holiday-themed pie pans appropriately shaped for pumpkin and apple pies. She created price stickers and reset a display, then added stackable pumpkins, pie pumpkins and a broad variety of squashes to the display. The Thanksgiving-themed corner was an ideal complement to the apple displays and the vintage tools Jax had hung on the back walls.

Call him. Say thank you. It's the least you can do.

A part of her wanted to. A part of her wanted to believe he was the real deal, an honest, hardworking man but honest men didn't hide their identities, especially when they represented the very company striving to take over her farm.

A farm that would soon belong to them

unless she fought it based on Gramps's diminished capacity which only made an ugly disease that much more unpalatable.

Text him, at least. He saved you hours of work.

She almost did it. She pulled out the phone and stared at the messaging app. Her finger hovered above it for three elongated seconds, then she slipped the phone back into her pocket.

Dishonesty had affected too much of her life. She simply couldn't risk being wrong again.

It was a nice thing for him to do and she couldn't deny the sigh of relief to see so much work done.

But she wouldn't call him or message him when the thought of him made her catch her breath. It was an absurd reaction to an impossible situation, but Mortie's words struck deep. Was she accusing him unjustly? Was it timing, and maybe even God's timing, that brought Jax up their road that day?

Of course not. Because why would he cover up who he was?

And that was what it came back to. He'd lied about his identity, and if he felt the need to mask that, there had to be a reason. The Ingersons didn't *need* more land.

They *wanted* more land. They were major kingpins of Washington State fruit, an industry that was pretty much controlled by a handful of producers as they swallowed up farm after farm in the Central Washington Valley.

Whatever Jax's motives were, she was pretty sure corporate greed ranked high on the list, because there was really no other reason for him to do what he did.

Wasn't there?

Their amazing kiss came instantly to mind.

Libby refused to think about that kiss. She reached behind the counter and turned the radio on. A country station filled the barn with background music, just enough to quiet her thoughts.

She might have to go up and down the rows she'd worked with Jax, and stand in the very spot where they shared that incredible kiss, but she didn't have to think about it. Not when country music offered an alternative, but when someone began crooning a love song about missing the dance, she reached over and turned the music off because she didn't want to hear anyone lamenting missed chances. Not when she might have missed the greatest one of all.

Chapter Eighteen

Jax chopped wood until the cabin stanchions overflowed with Douglas firs he'd dropped a few months before. Fortunately the cabin was tucked deep enough in the woods that he could cut and chop more if he wanted to. It was his hands-on therapy.

It didn't help.

Nothing helped. Even slipping into the barn to make sure Libby didn't overdo things seemed futile when he understood the pressure she was under.

Sleep eluded him. Peace evaded him, the peace he'd felt while working on the O'Laughlin farm. Among their trees.

Knowing that Libby was trying so hard to be so many things to so many people made him want to do better. Be better. Be healthy.

She didn't want him around her farm and her orchard. He understood that, but there was no way for her to handle the long work list on her own. They'd been barely covering the workload as it was. She couldn't juggle Cleve and CeeCee and the apple store for the rest of the season. He'd stayed out of sight all week, but he'd have to step in today. He'd driven by the apple store yesterday and saw how busy it was. Those numbers would be magnified for the weekend. And when Gert called to tell him she and two other drivers had come down with flu, he knew he had no choice.

He showed up at the apple store before it opened Friday morning. Libby pulled in two minutes later. She spotted him.

He wanted her to look happy to see him. Didn't happen.

She parked her hatchback on the far side,

climbed out and came toward him. "You can't be here."

"Where's Cleve?"

"Gramps isn't your concern, and no, I did not leave him home alone if that's what you're implying. Courtney is there."

He wasn't implying any such thing, but he let that go. She looked tired. No. *Exhausted* was a better word, and that was with his clandestine assistance.

"I'm here to help. It won't do you any good to argue, I have never left a job undone and I'm not about to start with this one. Not when it means so much to so many people I care about. We don't have to talk. We don't have to even see one another, but there's no way you can handle the rest of October on your own. There's no pay involved, no worries, no contact if that makes it easier for you," he told her. But while he had her attention, he needed to make one thing very clear. "And just so you know, CVF is not taking your farm. We never had any intention of taking your farm, and we consider that contract null and void due to your grandfather's diminished capacities. I don't know why he did what he did, but that signed contract was as much a surprise to us as it was to you. Now that's a whole other matter, but I wanted it cleared up. Here's my plan for today." He shoved his cap back slightly. "I'm going to restock the coolers and help move things over here. I know some of your help's come down sick and I'm not abandoning you with a three-day weekend at hand." A scheduled superintendent's conference day elongated this weekend. "You can put a call in to the sheriff's office if you want, have me dragged out of here, but it would be a lot easier if you just put blinders on and let me do my job. Which, for the next few weeks, is helping you."

Her eyes narrowed.

For a slow count of five, he wasn't sure what she was going to say, but then she squared her shoulders. "I can't pretend I don't need help right now."

Her admission took a weight off him. "I'll

keep my distance." That wasn't what he wanted to do, but what right did he have to court a woman like Libby when he had so much unfinished business of his own? "I'll start by bringing more Pinks and Braeburns over."

"That would be great. Yesterday's rain slowed down the few pickers we have this week."

Weather was a safe topic. He touched a finger to the brim of his cap, climbed into his truck and headed up the road. He purposely didn't look back, because if he did, he wanted to see her looking after him. Watching him.

If that wasn't the case, he didn't want to know. Right now she needed a friend to help her finish the season. If that's all he could be, he'd live with it.

He wouldn't like it.

But he'd deal with it, because for the first time in a long while, her happiness was more important than his.

And in an odd kind of way, it felt good.

* * *

"Gramps, you were amazing this weekend." Libby offered her arm to Cleve as they climbed the short flight of stairs into the kitchen on Monday evening. "I think we broke every record in the book, and I couldn't have done it without you."

"I know my apples," he boasted as they stepped into the kitchen.

"You sure do." CeeCee had dashed upstairs to get cleaned up. The quiet of the old house came as a respite after three days of nonstop work, but it was wonderful work. The very best. "Soup's ready. Why don't you have a seat and I'll bring some to you?"

"Sounds good. Smells better." He walked forward, a little stooped, as if too tired to hold his shoulders up.

She washed her hands, took the lid off the slow cooker and ladled piping hot soup for all of them. It needed to cool, so she loaded the dishwasher, then went and checked on Gramps.

She thought he'd fall asleep the minute he sat down.

He hadn't. He was sitting upright, and when she came into the room, he gave her a quick smile. "There's my Libby girl."

She took the quiet, cognizant moment and ran with it. Not because she wanted to, but because she needed to ask him about that signed contract. He might remember doing it. He might not, but O'Laughlin Orchards was *his* farm. His legacy. If he truly wanted to sell it, who was she to stand in his way? "Gramps, do you remember signing a contract for Central Valley Fruit?"

His expression went dark. His right hand thrummed a finger beat on the arm of his recliner. "I do what I have to do to take care of my girls."

His quick reply made no sense. She knelt down next to his chair. "You've always taken care of me, Gramps. CeeCee and I will be just fine, I promise, and we're so grateful for all you've done. You and Grandma blessed us in so many ways. We love you." She leaned over and gave him a hug. "But if you want to sell the farm, it's okay to do it. I just wanted to make sure that was your intention."

He grabbed her hand and held on tight. "This is your place, Libby."

She hesitated, confused, because did that mean he didn't mean to sign and send those papers?

"I don't want anyone fightin' you for anything, Libby. Not now. Not ever. When I'm gone, I'm gone, but if I just give you the money now, your mama can't say a thing. No one can say a thing. Your grandma will skin me alive if there's trickery around." His grip was strong and the concern in his voice matched his expression.

Her mother.

Had she approached Gramps? Or had just hearing her voice in the hospital pushed him to mail that contract? He'd wanted her to come. He'd made that clear to Mortie, but in his ramblings did he remember that? Did he see her as a threat?

She might never know, but at least now the signed documents made more sense.

"I don't want no one making trouble for you," he went on, and his voice grew more agitated with every word. "And if I have to sell the farm to do it, that's what we do. Your grandma and me had one hope. To make sure you came out okay. And you did." A sheen of tears brightened his eyes as he gripped her hand. "You surely did."

She hugged him. "No worries, Gramps. You don't have to sell the farm to take care of us. No one's going to bother us ever. I promise. You raised me to stand tall and strong and I won't disappoint you. Not ever again. I love you, Gramps."

He hugged her back.

He didn't do that often anymore. This time he did. And when he pulled back he sniffed the air. "That soup's smelling mighty good, ain't it? Ask Mother to bring me a bowl, would you? I'd be right grateful."

Evening fog was settling in outside and

in his mind, but she'd gotten the answer she needed. For whatever reason, real or imagined, he was trying to protect her from her mother's greed. She was sorry that he felt that need, but grateful for his faith in her. She'd lost faith in herself for a while.

Not now. And not ever again.

Libby noted the weekend's record sales in her online bookkeeping software on Tuesday morning and couldn't believe the numbers. At this rate, they might not be able to stay open until mid-November like she planned. She might be out of stock earlier than that, and wouldn't that be an amazing turn of events?

"I can't believe my whole class is coming here today!" CeeCee did her version of a happy dance as she skipped across the kitchen. "It will be the most fun ever!" She twirled twice, hands out, and almost knocked her mother's coffee to the floor. "Can I just have a cereal bar for breakfast, Mommy? My tummy is too excited to eat a lot of stuff and it's even more excited to come back here and eat donuts with my best and bestest friends!"

Libby had ordered dozens of donuts from Wenatchee. She'd need to pick them up once CeeCee was on the bus. Cleve wasn't up yet, so while CeeCee munched a granola bar, she crossed over to Gramps's room. She tapped softly on the door. "Hey, sleepy-head. You awake?" She peeked in the door. "Gramps?"

He was tucked into bed, snoring softly. One shoulder rose slightly, as if shrugging her off. She looked at her watch and frowned, but couldn't justify waking him to make a donut run. If he was tired out from the successful weekend, it was the best kind of tired ever. She closed the door softly and texted Jax.

Gramps is still asleep and I need the donut order picked up. Are you available? I'm on my own here.

Consider it done. Glaze Donuts?

Glaze Donuts was a popular donut shop in Wenatchee.

Yes. Gramps's favorite.

See you soon.

She put the phone away and walked CeeCee out to the bus. A chill wind had come through overnight, but the day's forecast was seasonally lovely, an ideal day for a field trip. She jotted a reminder to approach schools about field trips for the next year. Classroom outings would boost weekday business. If they could produce more of their own products for the next season, the thought of making a living wage off the farm was no longer a pipe dream.

She peeked in at Gramps. Still sleeping.

She grabbed a hoodie and a hat. When Mortie walked in the door a few minutes later, she walked out. "Gramps is still in bed, and I'm going to meet Jax at the apple barn and set up for the kids. Then I'll come back over here to meet the buses."

"In bed?" Mortie lifted a brow as she unzipped her sweater. "Not surprising after a three-day weekend at the apple stand. I'll check in on him and get some oatmeal going. He does love his oatmeal and brown sugar on cool mornings."

"With chopped apple." That had been a mainstay when she was growing up here. Others might have thought it to be a common thing, but to Libby, it was the best meal, anytime of day. "Call me if you need me."

"I will." Mortie slung her sweater over one of the kitchen hooks.

Libby crossed the drive and took the hatchback down the road. Jax pulled in about ten minutes later.

He looked wonderful.

She didn't want to think that. She didn't want to ponder knights in shining armor and heroes on horseback when he came around, but that was exactly what she did every time he showed up, only in a white pickup truck and a faded army cap.

He'd picked, wrapped, bagged and toted apples, cider, pumpkins and squashes all weekend. And when the crowds thinned late Monday afternoon, he began restocking everything with a little help from Cleve and more from the two pickers.

He moved her way with the strong, easy gait she'd come to know and probably admire too much. In his arms he held two commercial-size boxes of fresh donuts. "Can you get the door?"

Oh, man. She'd let the sight of him jumble her thoughts after she promised herself that wouldn't happen. "Of course." She swung the door wide. "I've got folding tables set up beneath the overhang. It should be nice enough by eleven to have donuts and cider outside."

"Then I'll set these there." He moved

through the barn and put the big boxes on the first table. Swaying branches whispered in the cool morning breeze. Leaves of bronze, rust, green and gold created a kaleidoscope of color against the clear blue sky. Backdropped by the orchard, Jax looked like an advertisement for the Washington fruit industry. A square-shouldered, rugged farmer, getting the job done day by day.

He slipped one box open and reached in. When he turned, he had a small wrapped pastry in his hand. He crossed the apple stand floor and held it out. "I'm going to guess you didn't stop for breakfast."

"Guilty. What did you—" She paused when she saw what he held in his hand. "One of their famous cinnamon rolls."

"Frosted," he noted, smiling.

Her favorite treat. She looked up. Big mistake because once she started gazing up, she didn't want to stop. "How did you know?"

"Cleve told me. I was hoping he was

right," he admitted with a slight smile. "His confusion could have made things interesting. Was he too tired to come over?"

"I think the weekend wore him out," she replied. "And, hey, I'll be happy to share that with you." She indicated the cinnamon roll. "That would save me half the calories."

"No can do," he told her. "A gentleman would have waited and eaten one with you, but I admit to wolfing mine down in the truck so I could get to work here. This one's yours. And I don't think calories are a problem." He gave her a cowboy kind of grin. "Not from where I'm standing."

Heat rushed into her cheeks as she reached her hand out. What could she say to that? Nothing that wouldn't get her in deeper, so she settled for the obvious. "Thank you."

He set the pastry into her hand with the merest touch of his palm to hers and it still felt wonderful. As if, somehow, they were connected. "You're welcome. Can't have the boss getting run-down, can we?"

The boss.

The words made her smile. "I can't deny I like being in charge. Even more because it's unexpected."

"Or maybe because you're really good at what you do," he supposed as he started to move away. She was a little annoyed that he didn't stay to flirt longer. But why would he when she'd sent him packing the week before?

He moved toward the coolers. "I'm going to restock here so you can meet the kids at the orchard when they come. Are the buses stopping there first?"

"Yes, then we'll come down here."

"Go ahead, then." He motioned toward the O'Laughlin house. "I've got this. We're looking good for today. And there was nothing nicer than to see Cleve's happy face all weekend, was there?"

Gramps had been in his element all three days. Smiling. Laughing. Helping folks to their cars with bags of fruit and jugs of cider. "It was the best," she admitted. "So if rain moves in now, or the weather turns, it doesn't matter because O'Laughlin Orchards had the best weekend ever and Gramps was a part of it."

"He sure was." He crossed the display area as she moved toward the door, and when his familiar whistle came back to her, she paused, smiling.

"Don't sit under the apple tree..."

The notes danced like the leaves on the autumn trees. As she backed up her little hatchback, her heart felt strong and good. They'd get through the busy season, get things straightened out with the farm and life would move on, but with one notable difference.

She and CeeCee were right where they should be. Home. On the farm.

"CeeCee, you live on the coolest place ever! Do you have any horses or cows?" Nathan Moyer skidded to a stop in front of

CeeCee and Libby two hours later. They'd tramped through the orchard, each child had picked an apple and now they'd gathered at the barn for snack time, consisting of cider and donuts. "I think farms always have horses and cows, right? Like black ones, maybe. Or brown, too."

"We don't even have *one animal*, Nathan," CeeCee explained in a despairing voice. Then she put her hands on her hips and sighed. "I can't even get a dog, like, just one big old dog to be my friend, so I don't think my mommy is going to buy me cows. And maybe they'd be too messy anyhow."

"And they would eat all of our apples and pears and we wouldn't have any to sell," Libby noted. "Cows need a lot of space and we've taken up most of our space with fruit trees. So that would be a problem, wouldn't it?"

"Then we can't ever, ever get a cow because we love selling apples so much, don't we?" CeeCee's eyes went round and she gave the apple store—*her apple store*, she liked to say—a quick look.

"Just like my gramps did when you were little and now you and me do it because we're family, right?"

"That's what makes it a family farm," said Jax as he drew close. "If you guys are all right here, I'm going to take my truck back up the road so we can load some more fruit."

"Thanks for showing us so much stuff, mister." Nathan clapped his hands together in excitement as he gazed up at Jax. "And for giving us donuts. They were really good!"

Jax palmed the little boy's head. "You're most welcome. Thanks for being such a good boy."

"Bye, Mr. Jax!" CeeCee gave him a quick hug as the teacher blew three soft *toot*s on a small whistle. "We've got to go back to school now. I'll see you later, okay?"

"Very okay."

"Is that gonna be your father, CeeCee?"

The petulant little girl from the classroom sidled up alongside CeeCee and Nathan. "Like, with your mom or something?"

"Just a good friend," Jax assured her. And as Libby's heart scrunched in her chest, he met her gaze across the trio of youngsters. "It's real nice to *have* a good friend and it's even better to *be* a good friend." He sent her a lazy smile, capped it off with a wink and walked away.

Oh, he was good. That hint of amusement and affection, just enough to draw her in. And she wanted to be drawn, which meant her resolve was weakening. Again.

"So you're never going to get a horse or a cow or maybe a pig?" Nathan seemed truly disappointed about the lack of animals. "Not even just one?"

Libby brought herself down to his level and smiled. "We're a fruit farm, Nathan. Like your grandpa used to have. This is actually your grandpa's barn."

The boy arched his brows, surprised. "When did my grandpa get a barn?"

"This used to be his farmland," Libby explained. "He sold it a few years ago but he kept this barn and let us borrow it."

"I didn't even know you could let people borrow buildings." The boy clapped a hand to his head, astonished.

The next toot on the teacher's whistle sent all three children rushing toward the waiting teachers. "Do we have something to say to Ms. Creighton?" asked CeeCee's teacher when they'd all gathered together.

"Thank you!" they shouted, then scrambled up the bus steps. Within five minutes the buses were rolling onto the road. Libby stood in the driveway area, waving goodbye. Samantha had come over to run the apple store so she could concentrate on CeeCee and the schoolkids.

Her phone suddenly buzzed. She ignored it until the last bus was up the road. Then she pulled her phone from her pocket to read the text.

The phone rang in her hand instead. Mortie's number appeared. And when she answered the phone, the nurse's voice meant business. "Cleve's slipping, Libby. Quickly, too. Come right home, honey. There's not much time."

Slipping?

He couldn't be. He'd been fine the past few days. Happy and more alert than usual and so excited to see the farm doing well. He couldn't be...

She swallowed hard.

Dying? Could he? Now? Today?

No.

She called out to Samantha, then raced to her car and made it up the road faster than she should have.

Jax was talking to Mortie. He saw her. The sadness on his face drove home Mortie's words. She skidded the car to a stop and jumped out. "What should we do? Call 911? Rush him in ourselves? What's the best thing to do, Mortie?"

Mortie looked at her. Looked at her real hard and real gentle all at once, and then she slipped an arm around Libby's shoulders. "Why, we let him go, darlin'. Same as we did your grandma last year. We sing him home on praise and worship and we remember the good times. Exactly the way he wants."

The way he wants. The DNR.

That couldn't be right.

The thought of doing nothing, of letting death have its day made Libby panic. Her heart thrummed. Her breath caught. But when she stepped into Gramps's room and heard the strained sounds of his breathing…

Libby paused. Then she walked over, drew up a stool and sat right there beside him to hold his hand, just like he'd done years before when make-believe monsters scared a little girl.

His eyes opened. She leaned in and kissed his old weathered cheek. "I love you, Gramps. So much."

He blinked. A hint of a smile touched his mouth, like the fledgling smile of a new-born child. "I took care of things," he whispered and gave her hand a weak squeeze. "All I could anyway."

"Shh." She laid her cheek against his. "You always did, Gramps," she whispered. "You always did."

His breathing evened out. His eyes drifted shut. When she lifted her cheek from his, peace softened his expression.

She sat on one stool.

Mortie made a couple of quiet phone calls, then brought a second stool in. And when Jax brought them each a mug of fresh hot coffee, he pulled up a third.

Mortie started humming.

They sang old hymns and a few new ones. "Amazing Grace," "Gather by the River" and "It Is Well with My Soul," one of Gramps's all-time favorites. When Mortie took the melody of "Leaning on the Everlasting Arms" and Libby joined with a soft alto, Gramps's troubled breathing went soft.

Softer.

And then stilled.

Libby was pretty sure her heart stopped beating right then, too. She clung to his hand, watching his color fade as his skin cooled. And then she laid her head against his chest one last time. There was no comforting heartbeat beneath her ear any longer. No strong arms came around to hold her, but they'd been there when she most needed them. Growing up. Trying to find the right path. Loving her through her mistakes and beyond. And now, after years of struggle, he was at peace.

His dream had come true. He'd had his final season, the most successful one of all and now he was home with his Savior. With his beloved Carolyn.

And while Libby was glad for his peaceful passing, part of her felt alone…so very alone…because the two people who loved her the way her parents never did were gone.

She knew they were safe in heaven. She believed that fully.

But she hadn't realized how dreadfully alone she'd feel down here on earth without them.

Chapter Nineteen

Jax toyed with canceling the Seattle therapy appointment on Thursday. It was a ninety-minute drive, then an hour-and-a-half session and ninety minutes back. An entire afternoon gone when Libby needed love and support.

He picked up the phone, then stopped himself.

He was doing so much better. Sleeping better and facing life straight on in so many ways. And now that his outlook was improving, it flickered a fire within him. He wanted to keep the momentum going. To be as whole and healed as he could be. This new therapy could be a part of that.

He studied the phone.

Was he afraid to keep the appointment? Yes.

Because what if it didn't work for him? What if he could never learn to trust himself again?

Go. You're the bravest of the brave. Go face what you must so you can live free. His therapist's words came back to him, urging him along.

That was what he wanted more than anything. To feel the weight lifted. To be himself again. And stay that way. Because how could he court a woman like Libby, or father an innocent child like CeeCee if he couldn't trust himself?

He sucked in a breath and texted Libby, Appointment this afternoon. I'll bring Chinese for supper, okay? The guys will finish picking today and crate everything into the cooler.

Supper's in the slow cooker. But fresh bread would be nice. CeeCee wanted to go to school.

There was an extended pause before the next text came in.

So I let her, but it's way too quiet here without her or Gramps.

Deafening silence. He understood that too well. She'd made arrangements for the funeral, and friends had gathered to help cover the apple store. They'd close it tomorrow out of respect for Cleve's death and reopen on Saturday. But the thought of her there, all alone, made his afternoon appointment an even more difficult choice.

Prayer time.

Jax had given up prayer for a long time. But sitting at Cleve's bedside praying in thought and song had reopened another spot inside him. A prayer spot, like when he'd pray with Grandma Molly, as if a gaping hole inside him had been filled.

Prayer time in the apple store, she texted back and her speed made him smile. Busy hands and an open heart. One of Grandma's favorite sayings.

She'd have loved Grandma Molly. See you tonight.

She sent a thumbs-up emoji.

He stared at it, torn. He wanted to be with her. Help her. Be her port in the storm.

But the what-ifs made him get in the truck and drive to Seattle. If this guy could make a difference in how Jax perceived that fateful day in the desert, it wasn't an afternoon lost. It could be a lifetime regained.

Libby was watering mums when the small SUV pulled into the gravel lot and parked. Samantha was taking care of customers inside the barn, leaving Libby free to get things done.

She turned as footsteps approached.

Her mother. Dianna. Here. Now.

The familiar adrenaline rush hit her. Her heart raced. Her fingers went cold.

Her mother looked around. Her gaze went from the fall displays to the line of apple-stocked tables inside. She sighed softly, then turned back. "This is beautiful, Libby."

That wasn't at all what Libby expected to hear.

"It's like he always dreamed it could be if he had a little more help. A little more time."

Libby heard the regret in her voice. Saw it in her face. But she was so tired of being fooled. She stayed silent and still, and knew it would make her mother the most uncomfortable. At that moment she didn't care.

"He wanted to make peace with me." Her mother's purse slipped off her shoulder. She hitched it back up. "It was a nice thing to do, but it agitated him to hear my voice. I could see that in the hospital and I'd already agitated him enough, I think. I never thought—" She sighed and paused, and her face reflected the sorrow in Libby's heart. *Seventy times seven.*

It was too much to ask. It was—

Let the one without sin cast the first stone. Christ's paraphrased instruction hit her squarely. She'd made her share of mistakes, and Grandma and Gramps had flung the door open wide to welcome her back. Her mother began to turn away. Libby's voice stopped her.

"That he'd go this soon."

"Yes." She turned back. Libby's response seemed to throw her a lifeline. "I thought I could come by after the apple season. Make amends. Catch him when he was feeling better, but it didn't happen. Now it never will. One more mistake to be sorry for." She drew a deep breath, adjusted her purse again, then stepped back. "I just wanted to tell you that. That I'm sorry for the mistakes, and I didn't want to make his time worse. But it was nice how he wanted me to visit. He didn't have to do that. But he did, and I'll never forget it." She began heading back to the SUV. The stoop of her shoulders reminded Libby of Gramps that last night. How he'd tried to lift others' burdens all his days. To stand tall and strong. A quality he'd passed on to her by example.

"Mom?"

Dianna turned.

"Please sit with us at the funeral tomorrow."

Her mother's brows drew down. Her chin quivered. "You want me there?"

"No." Libby took three steps forward, reached out and took Dianna's hand. "I *need* you there. All right?"

Dianna's hand trembled beneath hers. The shaking fingers testified to the difficulty in coming here. Facing Libby. "I'll come. Thank you."

"I'll see you then."

The school bus pulled up at the roadside. Gert was still out sick, but the substitute driver agreed to drop CeeCee off at the barn. The door swung open and CeeCee bounded out. "I made the best picture for

Gramps, Mommy!" She raced across the gravel drive and held up a very recognizable drawing of a tree. An apple tree. "My teacher helped show me how to do this and it looks just like a tree, doesn't it, Mommy? I think Gramps would love this tree so much, don't you?"

"Oh, he would, darling. It would be his favorite. And who is this?" Libby asked, pointing to a four-legged creature lolling beneath the tree.

"Dreamer! Dreamer wanted to be in Gramps's picture so I couldn't 'xactly say no, right?"

"He absolutely belongs there." Libby hugged her. "It's beautiful, CeeCee. Why don't you and Samantha hang it by the register?"

"Yes!" She skipped off, the image of a happy child.

Dianna followed her with a look of longing, then straightened her shoulders. "Can I meet her tomorrow? Instead of today? I'd rather tiptoe into her life than barge in uninvited."

Wise words. "Tomorrow it is."

Dianna left quietly. Libby watched her go.

She hadn't thought she'd find the grace of forgiveness within her, so why today of all days?

The Lord's Prayer, she realized. *And forgive us our trespasses as we forgive those who trespass against us...* Sage words for a peaceful life.

Libby joined CeeCee inside, and when they tacked the picture on the post behind the cash register, CeeCee beamed. "That's the best place for it right now. Where Gramps can watch us work from heaven, right?"

"Absolutely."

Libby watched CeeCee prance off to greet a new customer.

She'd made it this far pretty unscarred. Every now and again CeeCee wondered where her daddy went. Libby skirted that subject carefully, but all in all, CeeCee had been surrounded by love, just like the loving example Gramps and Grandma had set for Libby.

They closed up the apple store at six and drove up the road. When they pulled into the driveway, CeeCee hesitated. "It's kind of dark and lonesome, isn't it?"

Just then a light came on. Then another. And as they climbed out of the hatchback, Jax appeared in the doorway.

What would it be like to come home to someone like Jax every day? To love and cherish someone with such a good heart?

He deceived you. On purpose. Please don't pretend that doesn't matter.

It did matter, she realized, as she climbed the steps and saw the warmth in his eyes firsthand. But she'd never given him a chance to explain, so maybe she needed to back things up. She might be gullible, but the man standing in front of her didn't seem to have a dishonest bone in his body. Which meant she should give him a chance to come clean. If he still wanted to, that was. And after the way she'd treated him, she wasn't any too sure that would be the case.

Chapter Twenty

It was time to talk, Jax decided while Libby tucked CeeCee into bed. Not because he needed to clear his heart and maybe his soul, but because Libby deserved the truth. She came downstairs a few minutes later. When she spotted the kitchen, her eyes widened in appreciation. "I love a clean kitchen."

"I've noticed that. And yet you like to work in the kitchen. I expect you like to cook. Bake. Make things."

"Love it," she told him as she settled into the winged armchair. "Grandma was like that, too. When we're done making things, we clean the kitchen because a clean kitchen is an invitation to create."

He could see her doing that midwinter when the fields and orchards lay resting. He took a seat on the old sofa, opposite her. "Is this a good time to talk?"

Was it his imagination or did she look relieved? "Yes. Absolutely."

He folded his hands and leaned forward. "I haven't just been lying to you, Libby."

Her brows went up and the look of relief disappeared.

"I've stayed pretty much out of the limelight since I got back from Iraq." He folded his hands lightly, keeping himself slightly removed from the story he was about to tell. "I joined the army after college. I did it purposely, to give back to my country. I thought I understood the risks I would take. If God called me home, that was that. I never considered there would be consequences that went beyond death." He paused and stared down at his clenched hands. "Chalk that up to inexperience and youth, I guess."

She sat quiet and still, listening.

"My group was due to come home. We had six weeks left and we'd joke about what we were going to do first when we hit stateside. Kiss our girls, pig out on pizza, catch a dozen baseball games. So many plans." He never talked about this because just thinking about the guys choked him up. But tonight he was able to keep going for the first time since coming home. "I was pulled off a detail at the last minute for a meeting. Four of my guys went up as planned. Good men. And when I was almost back to base command, there was a funny sound. I looked up. And that chopper with four of my men on it was literally falling out of the sky. Just that. Falling, with nothing and no one to catch it. No one to stop the inevitable."

"Oh, Jax." She leaned forward. Sympathy deepened her voice and shadowed those pretty blue eyes.

He grimaced. "I watched it. In my head I've been replaying it for years, helpless to stop it." He paused, looked down, then lifted his eyes to hers. "I couldn't get over it. I think a part of me didn't want to get over it, as if my penance was to suffer forever. I stayed on the down low purposely. Didn't use my full name, lived alone in the woods and just made it through the days by doing odd jobs for people. My dad owns the cabin. He took care of the utilities and the therapist, and I coasted. I didn't want to die, but I felt like I didn't deserve to live. I was trapped between two worlds. And then I met you and CeeCee and Cleve and everything just clicked. Like a light bulb switching on. You needed help."

"We sure did." She offered a soft look of encouragement.

"And I was perfect."

She made a soft *hmm* but smiled.

He made a face. "I meant that I know fruits and orcharding. I know merchandising. My dad raised all of us with hammers and nails and power tools so we'd be able to tackle any job that came our way. And I'd seen my grandma through dementia. It was like God put me here at just the right time to help you because you guys needed each of those skills. And I had them. But you were so upset about CVF wanting to buy the place, that even when I had an opening to explain who I was, I didn't dare. Not just because you needed me." He glanced around the worn, cozy room. "Because I needed you—all of you—just as much. And I didn't want anything to jeopardize that."

She didn't just suspect the huge heart she'd sensed in him all along. She saw it. In his words, his expressions. She got up from the chair and took a seat next to him on the sofa. "I have a thing about lying."

He took one of her hands in his and held it.

"My parents were skillful liars. CeeCee's father followed that same vein and I fell for it completely. It wasn't until I ended up in the ER and found myself lying about how I got a concussion and a bruised face that I realized I was becoming part of the problem. I went into a shelter with CeeCee. He took all of our money and left me destitute and homeless. Then he filed for a divorce I was happy to give him at the same time Grandma and Gramps needed our help."

"Libby, I'm sorry." He drew her in then. Into the safe curve of his arm, and drew her head down to his shoulder. "So sorry. No one should have to go through that."

"Folks go through a lot of things," she whispered. "It's how we handle the aftermath that makes us who we are. At least, that's what Grandma used to say." She leaned back and peeked up at him. "So what now?"

He winced, which wasn't exactly the expression she hoped to see. "Well—"

She nudged him with her right elbow. "In the movies, this is where the hero and heroine kiss and you know that they're going to have the happy-ever-after they both deserve."

"Except what happens to the happy ending if the hero wakes up screaming in the middle of the night?"

She drew back. Faced him. And put her hands gently on his cheeks. "Then the heroine holds him and tells him everything will be all right. And after a while, it will be. And they go on to sell lots of apples and maybe have a baby or two and name one of them Cleve. If it's a boy, that is, because Cleveland is a silly name for a girl. That's how I see this going down anyway. So how about you, soldier?" She met his gaze full on, deliberately. "How do you see this unfolding?"

"Like this." He kissed her. And when he was done, he held her close in his arms. "Are you willing to take a chance, Libby?"

"Is that your idea of a proposal?" She made a face at him and he laughed.

"Libby Creighton, would you do me the honor of becoming my wife? The honor of working in orchards and raising little kids into fine adults and being with me through the good times and the bad?"

"Much better." She peppered his face with kisses. "I will, Jax. I'll marry you and be your partner and hopefully raise a few cute kids together. But on one condition."

"Proposals don't come with conditions. Do they?"

"This one does. I want to keep this farm as a tribute farm to the original settlers here. The first fruit growers in Central Washington, the ones who began it all, including your family and mine. I don't want it to become part of the huge Ingerson CVF. I want to build that barn or maybe just buy Moyer's barn and have folks come and enjoy a reasonably priced farm experience every year. It won't step on CVF's toes, and I think in the end it would be a blessing to so many folks."

"*That's* your condition?"

"Well, it's not a deal breaker," she answered, "But—" She kissed his right cheek.

Then his left. And then his mouth. "It would make your wife very, very happy."

"You strike a hard bargain but a fair deal. I think that's a brilliant idea actually. Because coming to the barn makes people happy and seeing them happy made me happy, too."

"Me, too. Jax?"

"Mmm-hmm?"

"I love you. I absolutely, positively love you. Just the way you are."

His arm tightened around her. He drew her in again, but not for a kiss this time. For a hug. A hug that felt like coming home, at long last. For both of them. "I love you, too." He stood and drew her up with him. "But as much as I'd like to keep right on holding you, we need sleep. Tomorrow we say goodbye to a wonderful man."

"And hello to a new beginning. Gramps would approve."

"I believe he would. Walk me to the door, darlin'. Then tomorrow we'll take Gramps on his final walk on earth…"

"While he gathers with Grandma and friends in heaven."

"Amen to that." He kissed her one last time and went out the side door.

She watched him jog to his truck. Strong, virile, handsome…and wounded, just like her.

But together they would bind those wounds and stand strong. And the fact that they could do it and keep the O'Laughlin name alive made it sweeter. She hadn't wanted to say goodbye to Grandma or Gramps, ever. Now that she had, she wanted their name, their legacy, to be respected, and her future offered her the chance to do that.

And that was a blessing she never expected.

Epilogue

"**W**ell, sweet thing, you surely did get a perfect day for a wedding." Mortie adjusted Libby's gown from behind. "I've never seen a more beautiful day in late November. And aren't you the prettiest thing?" She smiled at Libby through the mirror, then kissed Libby's cheek. "I am honored to help you today. I hope you know that."

"I do."

CeeCee sashayed in, and her swishy skirt splayed out as she spun. "I can't even believe how pretty this dress is, Mommy, and yours is so pretty, too! Won't Mr. Jax and his dad and the uncles think we're just the prettiest things ever?"

"I'm sure Jax will feel that way, but your new aunties might take exception. Are we ready?"

"We are." B.J. Johnson went to the side door and opened it wide. "Your chariot awaits, ladies."

She walked out, expecting B.J.'s SUV to be in the driveway.

It wasn't.

A Cinderella-style carriage stood in the farm drive, with four big broad horses standing strong and tall in front.

"B.J." She turned as CeeCee let out a little squeal of delight. "Jax did this?"

"I am not at liberty to say who did what, but I think you can figure it out."

A soft *woof* came from the front seat of the carriage, next to the tuxedo-wearing driver. And then a shaggy black-and-white dog poked a head up, over the edge. He spotted her. Then CeeCee. And his mouth opened in a doggy smile as his tail slapped a rhythm against the carriage driver's seat.

"Oh, you have a nice dog!" CeeCee hurried out the door and stared up at the dog and the driver. "He's so beautiful, mister!"

"I have no dog, miss." The driver turned. *Jax.*

Sitting up there, all handsome and happy and maybe a little smug.

"I do believe this dog belongs to a young lady who lives at this very house. Someone named Cecelia, I believe?"

CeeCee's mouth gaped open. "Dreamer?"

Jax reached out and flipped a small sign attached to the dog's collar. "Yep. Dreamer."

Libby's heart nearly burst.

She couldn't have thought to make this day any better, nicer or sweeter, but Jax just did. "Up you go, miss." B.J. offered her a hand into the carriage. And when he tried to do the same for CeeCee, she aimed a pleading look at Jax up front. "Can I ride with you and Dreamer, Mr. Jax? I'll be so good!"

"How is your mother going to feel about

dog hair on your dress, sweetness? Check with her."

The absolute look of love on CeeCee's face evaporated dog hair worries. How often did a little girl get to be a real, live princess in a carriage? Libby nodded and gave CeeCee a princess-style wave. "See you at the church, darling."

He didn't drive the horses quickly. He let them meander up the road. Folks came out of their houses and waved and laughed and cheered. As they drew into the small town of Golden Grove, people lined the short sidewalks or stood on porches, calling out congratulations.

Libby had left the town in shame long years ago.

She'd come back, ready to remove the tarnish from the family name, but as she stepped out of the carriage and put her hand into Jax's, the happy smiles around her taught her a real lesson.

Most folks didn't care what happened twenty years ago. They rejoiced in the here and now, with her. With Jax. With CeeCee. On this beautiful day, surrounded by so many people, the whole town seemed like it was wishing them well.

"Ready?"

She turned to Jax as CeeCee skipped ahead once they'd convinced the dog to stay in the carriage. "Absolutely."

They started forward. At the last minute, just before they got to the open church doors, Dreamer jumped down, bounded forward, dodged around them and went to stand sedately at CeeCee's side.

He didn't bark.

Didn't whine.

He just stood there, and when CeeCee started down the aisle, so did the dog.

"Should I get him?" Jax whispered. "This wasn't part of the plan."

Libby watched the dog and little girl walk down the aisle, then she looked up at him—her soon-to-be husband—and smiled. "I know the plans I have made for you." She paraphrased the quote from Jeremiah and squeezed his arm lightly in a silent message.

"God's plan it is." He grinned down at her and when the music started, he walked her down the aisle to a future neither one had seen coming. A future filled with hopes and dreams for two people who'd weathered storms and emerged. And when he promised to love, honor and cherish her for all of his days...

Libby Creighton knew that it was true.

* * * * *

If you loved this story,
be sure to pick up Ruth Logan Herne's
previous miniseries,
Shepherd's Crossing:
Her Cowboy Reunion
"Falling for the Christmas Cowboy"
from A Cowboy Christmas
A Cowboy in Shepherd's Crossing
Healing the Cowboy's Heart

Available now from Love Inspired!

Find more great reads at
www.LoveInspired.com.

Dear Reader,

I enjoyed writing this story because we all have so much to thank the Lord for, even in hard times.

I love blending faith and romance, and I love adding children into stories because they are the hope for the future. But Cleve was a big part of my love for this story.

The road of Alzheimer's and dementia is not easy. It is nothing to be undertaken lightly. The scourge of Alzheimer's runs in my husband's family. His father, his grandfather, his uncles and all of his great-uncles had it. That makes this a personal experience for us as a new generation tiptoes into that age group.

I hope you loved Libby and Jax's story. It was inspired when I read about this new treatment for PTSD developed by Frank Bourke to help post-9/11 victims. His work has been refined to help returning soldiers. When I read the positive results of the clinical trials, I saw my hero, Jackson Ingerson. The brain's a funny thing. When one moment replays in our heads incessantly, it can mess with our emotional stability until we learn how to hit that mental off button without guilt.

Libby's story hits close to home for me and so many people who come from dysfunctional families. It's hard to live your life categorized by others' actions, isn't it? But she learns and rises above, and I just love her.

Thank you so much for reading this story. I love hearing from readers. You can email me at loganherne@gmail.com or through my website, ruthloganherne.com, and I love it when folks follow my friends page or author page on Facebook!

God bless you all, and I hope you love all of the Golden Grove, Washington, books.

With love,
Ruthy